THE DEAD LAND GIRL

THE DEAD LAND GIRL

JOHN JOHNSON

Troubador Publishing Ltd
Unit E2 Airfield Business Park,
Harrison Road, Market Harborough,
Leicestershire LE16 7UL
Tel: 0116 279 2299
Email: books@troubador.co.uk
Web: www.troubador.co.uk

ISBN 978-1-83628-055-2

British Library Cataloguing in Publication Data.
A catalogue record for this book is available from the British Library.

Printed and bound in Great Britain by 4edge Limited
Typeset in 12pt Adobe Jensen Pro by Troubador Publishing Ltd, Leicester, UK

To Ella, Joseph, Lucy and all, and to Aunt Kath, without whom this would have been unlikely.

FOREWORD

Many lives were changed for ever in that summer of 1940, not just mine. Lives were lost, airfields attacked, homes destroyed, factories and workplaces burned down. The Expeditionary Force was defeated, and just barely transported home. I've tried in this account to capture the moments that changed my life, but I do not know which was most significant: the moment I encountered a senior detective, perhaps; my visit to a funeral parlour, quite possibly; the late-night stumble in the farmyard, one of the worst moments of my life, so a good possibility; the RAF pilots calling to us over the hedge – that led to changes, certainly. But perhaps the moment I was shoved down my particular path through the wood came in that dingy drill hall....

CHAPTER 1
JUNE 3RD 1940

"Me? A Land Girl? Why on earth would I want to be a Land Girl?" I couldn't help reacting. His suggestion was so outrageous. I'd never thought of becoming a Land Girl. That was just making up for the absent farm labourers. Surely I had more to offer than that? But my heart had sunk a little even as I'd entered the wretched drill hall they were using for the recruitment interviews, and the recruiting officer in front of me, a despondent looking weed of a man, would hardly inspire anyone to devote their lives to the service of their country. I should have anticipated that the interview would go wrong.

I thought I had better say something to fill the silence, because he was obviously stuck for words. "I know the continent of Europe well, I've lived most of my life there rather than in Britain, but I am British, and my father has done and is doing great service for our country. I can speak both French and German fluently, and Polish of course. I can drive a car or a van, I can shoot a rifle, do I need to go on and add more? You know that I have skills that can be useful. Why do you want to send me to some farm to dig ditches?" I tried to smile a little, and look begging, which works with most men – but I wasn't sure it was working here.

He seemed almost apologetic as he finally spoke. "Miss Beauchamp," he pronounced it Beecham, as it should be pronounced, and I guessed that he had heard of my father, and so of me, before, "if it was just me deciding this, I might be tempted to take a chance on you and look at the auxiliary services. But even if I approved your application, it would be stopped at the next stage by those who monitor the applications."

So that was it! He had some fear of his superior officers. But why would they want to turn me down? I had not expected this. I was thinking of doing some brave and heroic work for the war cause, not hiding in the countryside fending off the advances of the local farmers. "Why?" I protested, still trying to catch his eyes directly to persuade him to change his mind, but he looked down at his papers again. "Why would your invisible superiors stop my application?"

"Because you've failed your medical. The doctor won't sign you off as fit for the services." Now that shocked me. Of all the things that I had thought, hoped or feared might happen to me, none of them included failing the medical. The doctor had only listened to my chest and heartbeat, and checked that I could raise my hands in the air, touch my toes and lift a weighty medicine ball. So I stood up, stretched out my arms and circled them just as the medic had asked me to. "I am completely fit. I play tennis, swim, ski, and walked in the mountains in Europe until we had to leave and come back here."

"I'm aware of that. But indeed your life in Europe may be responsible for the doctor's opinion. He…" He hesitated and looked up at me and then back again at his papers, but I was no longer prepared to try to persuade him by fluttering my eyes. This was more serious. "He suggested that you had had tuberculosis. It means you are ineligible for the auxiliary services. No-one who has had TB is allowed to sign up. It can reoccur and is contagious."

Now I was shocked. TB was associated with poverty, both in Britain and on the continent, though I was aware that some of our Romantic poets and other writers and artists had died of consumption, a euphemism for TB. "TB, TB? No, that can't be right. No-one ever told me that. I don't remember ever being told that."

"But perhaps you may remember at some point in your childhood being unwell for a period of time, or maybe you were sent up into the mountains to breathe better. I can only tell you what the doctor has said. I'm sorry."

Oh God! That struck a chord. I had been unwell when I was six or seven, and my mother had taken me to stay in a hotel in the mountains. Or rather, she called it a hotel. I was not going to give up though. "How can I prove my fitness? I'm sure I can get this overturned." Surely, I was thinking, my father would be able to pull some strings and get me a proper role in the war effort?

"You might," he said, "but there are other matters that my superiors, as you call them, would react to."

For goodness sake, I thought, what else can there be? "What? What matters? What are you talking about?"

"Your school records, I'm afraid. It seems you were … you were expelled from two schools." Well, that was true, but they were silly incidents. In the first, two of us had distracted the chemistry master, who was an utterly hopeless teacher, while a third had put a small flask of petrol into the container he was about to heat up. The fire had mostly burned his white coat, not him. As for the second, well you can't keep a whole gaggle of sixteen-year-old girls locked up forever, can you?

"But those were trivialities," I protested, but he ended my protest by raising his hand.

"And a brush with the Metropolitan Police, and the magistrates. That they would not ignore."

"But it was just a misunderstanding," I said, but inwardly I cursed my friends' liking for alcohol and for urging me to drink more.

"You would need many positive things to support you in trying to overturn a medical. These things are not positive. I'm sorry."

I was crestfallen and did not reply. I really did not like the thought of being shoved onto a farm for the duration of the war, especially now as it looked so bad and everyone was afraid it was going to be longer and bloodier than the

Great War. And I could not work out why no-one had told me about the TB, except to think that maybe it would seem like a fault of theirs if either my mother or father had admitted it to me.

The recruiting officer spoke again. "Look," he said, "the farms in Essex are desperately short of labour. They've already lost a lot of men to the armed services, and now the government is making many of them plough up pastureland and grassland to plant cereals and vegetables. It's more efficient, you see, but it's also more labour-intensive. Crops need workers out in the fields, whereas cows just need milking morning and night. You would be close to home and to your father, and if you served for… let's say a year… there might be a much better chance of the WAAF authorities looking at you and your skills in a better light." He seemed to know a lot about me, or rather I guessed he knew about my father and had found some additional information about me. I remained silent. I did not want to capitulate, though I could see the sense in what he said. I did want to serve, and the country could hardly be in a worse state than it was in, with the Expeditionary Force barely rescued from Dunkirk and France toppling before the German onslaught.

"So what do you want to do, Miss Beauchamp? Shall I write out the referral. It's not a conscription, you know. You can take a referral away with you and use it or not, according to your decision."

"Alright," I muttered. "Yes, write out a referral. I need to speak to my father about all this." I tried my hardest to smile, though part of me felt like crying. I would much have preferred to speak to my mother about it first. She, after all, was the one who had taken me away to that hotel, or sanatorium as I now guessed it had been. But that was not possible. She had decided, against every entreaty first of my father, and then of mine, to stay in Poland and try to protect her people on her estate. That was the last we had heard of her. I knew it was not just a futile gesture. The people there would indeed look to her to try to protect them when the invaders arrived, and she would make that attempt unflinchingly. But she had disappeared behind what was now a wall of silence, and communications from the underground in Poland had almost dried up and would not concern themselves with events so far from the major cities. I had no hope of talking to her about my situation. So, my father it had to be.

I took a bus to Westminster from the recruiting office. Was it just me, or were people subdued by events in France? There seemed to be a slightly astonished look on everyone's face, as if they had just seen something so wholly unexpected as to overturn their trust in normality. But then, I thought, I had the benefit, not that that's the right word, of having seen the speed of the Germans' attack in Poland, of going from a peaceful, ordered existence to one of war, of bombs, of frightening planes in the sky, and of a cowed populace suddenly realising the scale of the forces unleashed on them. I had not been surprised by events in France. And nor had my father. The moment news broke of the first German thrusts through the forests, he'd packed as much

6

as he could in the car and we – I, he and his butler-come-assistant Henri – had fled across Italy and France with as much speed as we could, sleeping in the car and exhausting his ready cash as we paid the increasingly high charges for petrol. The Riley we had to leave on the quayside, having sold it to a garage owner in Bordeaux at a knockdown price, before boarding a British boat headed to the South Coast. But we had certainly understood the power and might of the Germans. Now my fellow countrymen and women had learned of it as well.

My father's office was not in the Foreign Office itself. Relations with the Polish government-in-exile and other East European exiles had been downgraded after the country had been overrun. If he'd been in liaison with the French, or even better the Americans, he would have been based in one of those swanky rooms, with leather-backed chairs and red-cushioned armchairs and sofas, but instead he was in a mundane office block nearby, though he did at least have decent views of Westminster Palace and Big Ben through the grubby window. I was ushered into his office fairly quickly, the staff having become used to my regular visits which always started in the same way. "Any news?" I would ask hopefully. "No, none," he would answer more neutrally, "though that's not necessarily a bad thing." We would lapse into silence for a while, as we each pondered the implications of there being no news. But this time I followed it up. "If mummy had been here," I said, "I would have asked her about my having had TB."

He looked up from the papers he had been continuing to skim through despite my presence. "TB, Ginny? TB? What's that about?" I looked him in the eyes trying to determine if his surprise was genuine, but as on many previous occasions I could not read his look. He was too accomplished a diplomat, an entrepreneur, a leader. He could not be easily read. "Who's said anything about TB?"

"Just the doctor at my medical." I spoke rather sharply, as if I were reprimanding him, even though I did not know if a reprimand were deserved. "They've refused me for the WAAF because I've previously had TB. I didn't know." I left out the two expulsions and the Magistrates' Court. I didn't want to hear "I told you so" just at this moment. I wanted to see if my sudden announcement would crack the façade of my father's usual insouciance. But he showed no sign of any such fracture.

"Is that what the doc said? Could he be wrong? Though, there was that time your mother took you up into the mountains…" His words ran out, but he had hit the same notion as I had earlier. "She told me you'd had a chest infection, but that it healed up in the mountain air. Perhaps I should have questioned it more, but your mother could cover things up so efficiently that if she wanted to conceal it from me, she would. She didn't tell you?"

The question was hypothetical. He knew the answer. "Told me it was a hotel, and that we were taking the waters, I think that's the phrase she used. Never mentioned it again."

"Do you want to see a specialist?" My father had a somewhat naïve belief in specialists. He thought they could do things other doctors couldn't, not just charge you ten times the normal rate for treatment, which they always did. I shook my head. It wouldn't do any good.

"They offered me the Land Army," I said quietly. "Told me to think about it. Maybe I could prove I am really fit by serving there. It's not what I wanted."

"No, it wouldn't be. You've served some time on the farms in Poland, haven't you, on orders? Probably enough to put you off for life." His look was slightly sad, as if he were regretting allowing my mother to play the dominant role in my upbringing and education. "What will you do?" His tone was gentle, and he was clearly trying not to influence me either way.

"I suppose things are so bad that I feel I must do it. I can't just sit around and listen to the news. I've got to feel that I'm doing something."

"I could try to get you a job in administration of some kind, but the truth is…." Again his speech ran out. It didn't need saying. I had never administrated anything, couldn't type, and wouldn't know a filing system if I fell in the middle of it. I was not going to be an administrator. I needed to do something, but not that.

"They said I'd be based in Essex, so I'd be able to get back and visit you. Maybe it won't be as bad as I fear." Whistling in the wind, I think they call it. "I'll go home now and have a chat with Henri, and tomorrow I'll probably go and register." Henri, my father's former batman, and now butler, driver, assistant, chef, caretaker, but above all his friend – he would at least tell me if what I was about to do was completely unwise. But having listened to my plight, and confirmed that my father had never mentioned my having TB, indeed nor had my mother, he simply asked, "Was it the expulsions from school?" I nodded and mumbled something about the magistrates as well. "Then I think you've made a good decision," he said.

CHAPTER 2
JUNE 4ᵀᴴ-17ᵀᴴ 1940

I had to go to Oxford Street to register for the Land Army and to obtain my uniform. My mother had taken me shopping there on previous visits to London, and I had enjoyed the shops, but the same gloom that was affecting everyone had descended even there. The windows were depressing, and some were already boarded up; the shop workers were depressed, and the customers were the cause of their depression. The sparkle that I remembered from December shopping expeditions had completely disappeared, and though it was summer it felt like November. The Land Army had taken over a property on Oxford Street, and while I was there other young women were also joining up, obtaining uniform, or enquiring about joining. They were giggling with friends or relatives about their appearance in the unfamiliar clothes or making jokes about how they'd always wanted to work with animals. It seemed just about the busiest and happiest place in the West End, and I was buoyed by their good spirits in a way that the recruiting officer, for example, or indeed my father had failed to do. Perhaps a year's rural penance would not be so bad in the company of some of these cheerful young women.

I showed my referral to the first clerk I met, and she pointed out where I should sign up by putting my signature on a pledge. This required me to acknowledge that I was signing up for the duration of the war, to abide by the conditions of training and employment, and to make the home fields my battlefield. I would promise to serve well and faithfully. The reverse of the card indicated that resignation was possible but required permission. I hesitated. I hadn't thought that the commitment might be so long. We were already nine months and more into the war, and it did not seem likely to end for many more. The Great War had lasted over four years. "Everything okay?" the clerk asked me. I smiled and signed, though perhaps in my mind I was holding my nose, or crossing my fingers, or in some other way reminding myself of my uncertainty and anxiety. "Have you worked on a farm before?" she asked. "Only some of the women coming in here have never seen a cow or a pig, never lifted a shovel, never worked in the sunlight."

I nodded. I had worked on a farm. Indeed I had worked on a few. After my second expulsion my mother had said nothing to chastise me. She had just packed her bags and mine and left the city within twenty-four hours of my return from school, and we had travelled together to her estate. So part of my punishment was to be denied any access to my friends. I understood that. But when we got there she said to me, "Come downstairs in the morning in your oldest clothes. You're going to work on one of the farms." I've read somewhere that a bishop's church is called a cathedral because the bishop speaks with authority from his cathedra, his seat. Sometimes my mother's pronouncements were like that, authoritative, undeniable. Through experience I had learned not to react against such utterances, though at other times when she did not speak "ex cathedra" I knew that there was scope to argue, reason or plead my case. Not then, though. So next day I had put on an old sweater, some worn-out jodhpurs and black boots. I thought I looked a little like Coco Chanel, though the staff in my mother's house smiled when they saw me.

And so through June, July, August and part of September – until the harvest was in – I had worked from eight until six every day except Sunday on a variety of farms around the estate. The farmers and their labourers had to show me how to herd and milk cows, to rescue small piglets from under their swollen mothers, to hoe the fields, to pollinate and cull the fruit, to shoo the birds, filch the honey from the bees, to dig ditches , kill the rats and other vermin and all the other work that went on. The cows kicked my shins, the pigs knocked me over in the filth, the bees stung me, the thorns pricked me, and once a ditch collapsed on me and almost buried me. I had aches where I'd never known I had muscles, and blisters on my feet and hands that burst and turned raw. It took me a while to work out why I was doing all this manual labour and suffering so much. I concluded that my mother was annoyed with me for what I had done, but particularly because I was showing too casual and disregarding an outlook on my life and future. She wanted to demonstrate to me how hard life really was, and how we all had to work hard and work together to do important things. And that hard work was rewarding in itself. I think it took me around two months to understand the conversations we had over dinner after each of my working days, and so understand what she had meant me to understand. And then came the hardest lesson of all.

I knew that when she was in the house at the centre of the estate my mother was often called on to act as an extra midwife. She had some medical training in the latter years of the War, and had continued to apply it when necessary at home. During that summer three children were born on farms around the estate. And each time my mother took me with her to the births. Other local women would also appear, summoned by some communication system of which I was unaware, and they would muster around the bed of the soon-to-be mother and apply their collective wisdom and experience. I was allowed to gather the boiling water, to bring fresh towels, to serve the dark tea which they all drank as their only nourishment during the last hours of these labours. My mother had obviously feared that my sneaking out of the school at night with my friends showed me to be at risk morally, and so my presence at these rituals was intended to show me what could happen if I continued to behave so riskily. The screaming and shouting of those in labour, the prompting and urging of the coven of midwives around the bed, the sweat and blood that had to be wiped up, the silent anxiety of the men-folk gathered in the rooms below – well, they were simply the best education about sex and its consequences that a sixteen-year-old like me could receive. After the third, a particularly long-drawn-out labour in which the woman cried continuously for hours on end, I vowed to myself that I would remain chaste for life. No man was going to put me through that!

I wiped a tear from my eye. Why did thinking about my mother make me cry every time? The clerk was looking at me a little askance. She leaned forward kindly and said, "You okay? You seemed for a moment …."

"Yes I was," I muttered, "I was thinking of something else for a moment. Sorry."

"Go over to the counter now, hand in the pledge card and they will start a file for you. Then you will be able to get the uniform and after that you'll get a letter telling you when and where to report." She gave me a sympathetic smile, and for a moment I almost blurted out why I'd been crying, but I thought some self-restraint was probably better, and I smiled back and followed her pointing finger.

The referral had recommended Essex for my destination, and that was noted along with my pledge card, which was given a number. The uniform, parts of which I had to purchase, was quite the most undignified and ugly clothing I had ever been given. I could no longer hesitate –

I'd signed up. But if I'd seen in advance what I would look like – well, I might have volunteered for munitions work instead, which everyone knew was the most dangerous and unhealthy, and possibly short-term, of all the jobs the government now thought it appropriate for women to undertake. At least the women on the newsreels didn't all look like frumps as they lugged shells and dynamite across their factory floor. Coco Chanel I was not!

I walked home through the parks. Normally it was a walk that would lift my spirits, especially now that the weather was warming. But I still had mixed feelings about what I had committed myself to doing. Around Victoria the newsboys were shouting their headlines about the fall of France, but people were not rushing to buy the papers. They'd had too much bad news recently. But the idea that France had been so quickly and comprehensively overrun reminded me of all the reasons why it was right to do something to fight back, and it put a certain steel into my resolution to do my best in this new role.

When I got home I found Henri and my father packing bags and turning out some food and bottles of wine and spirits. "What's going on?" I asked. "Where are you going?"

"To Leicestershire, for a long weekend. I've been asked to do a new job, a quite different job to what I've been doing for the Foreign Office, so I'm going to see the estate and visit the farms while I can before I start next week. Want to come? You'd better get packing if you are."

I didn't wait to question him about the new role. I hurried to my room and threw things into the largest case

I could lay my hands on. I didn't pack anything fancy. I knew my father would drive with Henri from one farm to another for most of the time, and he would not be hosting any dinner parties or social gatherings. The bottles of drink were intended mostly as presents for various estate staff. But I would be able to enjoy the large grounds of the big house, and if I accompanied my father I would see at close hand some of the work I too was about to undertake. So heavy shoes and light clothing, sufficiently modest for visiting farms. An easy pack.

I waited until Henri had cleared the London suburbs to question my father about the new job. I need to tell you a little about him first though. He was born into a wealthy land-owning family. His brother joined up on the first day of the Great War and was killed two years later on the Western Front. He joined up that same year, and he too served on the Western Front. But he had studied languages, and as the War finished he was transferred to eastern Germany and then to Poland to help train up the new army there and to assist the new country in establishing itself. Somewhere along the way he acquired Henri, who devoted himself to quietly assisting my father in all possible ways. He met my mother, who I suppose was from a similar background, owning land and having inherited a title. They married and my father left the army and set up a business importing cars through ports such as Danzig, and also building them from kits which came in large containers. He sold the cars all over Poland, and the business thrived. I was born, and my parents settled into a life moving between their two estates, the one in Poland and the other in Leicestershire, and a variety of cities in Poland where my father had garages selling and servicing the cars. He knew the ambassador to Poland in the 1930s, and did various tasks for him, which made him some kind of honorary consul, and he got to know members of the Polish government. He warned them of the powerful forces that Hitler was creating, and they tried to heed his warning, but the Polish forces were still overwhelmed by the planes and tanks that attacked them in September 1939. That's when we started to flee south, but my mother would not leave her land and people. I can remember my father saying to her that if it was just the Germans, he could understand her. They were evil but were probably inclined to leave estate lands in the hands of the owners if they caused them no problems. But even if we win the war, he warned her, it's not likely we would get to you before the Russians. They will not leave the lands in the possession of landowners. They will not be at all sympathetic to you. But none of his arguments prevailed, nor mine about how much I needed her, and I hugged her and kissed her and witnessed their last embrace before we hurried away in the car.

My father explained that he was impatient to start some new work. The Polish government-in-exile was important, but he did not think they really understood the reality of their situation. He didn't say it was hopeless, but it was clear that that was what he implied. He had told the British government of his considerable experience in the motor industry, and they had now given him a key role in co-ordinating the production of aircraft, establishing new factories, employing and training staff, getting parts manufactured and the planes assembled. That was all he could tell me, but it would mean that he would not be in London much, if at all. I was delighted for him. It seemed a role that he was so well-equipped to carry out, since he had done all that and more with the cars that he had sold in Poland, and I sensed in him the urgency of the task for the good of the country. He had cleared his desk in the course of a single afternoon, briefed his colleagues about the various tasks in which he had been involved, and agreed to take two and a half days off before starting the new role the next week. He was sorry that I would not see him much in the future, but I could still use the apartment in Victoria when I wanted. It was a good thing that I was starting my own work elsewhere and would be occupied. He lapsed into silence, and I knew why. If we weren't occupied doing something, we would both think of my mother, and wonder how she was, what she was doing, what life was like under occupation. It was indeed better to be doing something, anything, than thinking for too long in that way.

CHAPTER 3

JUNE 22ND, 23RD AND 24TH 1940

The two and a half days we spent in Leicestershire were glorious, sunny days, and I shall remember them as our last happy days before the war effort took over all our lives. The estate house and the roads and farmhouses were all much as I remembered them, but the landscape had already changed considerably. I discovered that as soon as war had broken out my father had sent instructions to the estate managers to alter the whole nature of the estate and the farms. Grassland and pastureland had either been ploughed up or was marked out for ploughing after the harvest. The large numbers of sheep and cattle had diminished considerably, and the first crops of wheat and barley, onions, carrots, potatoes and other vegetables were growing towards a summer harvest. Even the big lawn in front of the house had been ploughed, and leeks were growing there. Some of the woods had been cut down and sold for mine props or fuselage. New ditches to aid the drainage had been dug. But my father had said, "We're in the same position as the rest of the country. Too much work to do and too little labour left. We'll be employing the Land Army here in a month's time." I wondered if I had made a mistake in allowing myself to be assigned to Essex. Perhaps I should have committed to working in Leicestershire, but then I thought that might prove difficult and socially awkward. Better Essex, where I was unknown, and from where I could always escape to the London flat.

Two days after my return, and with my father and Henri already disappeared to who knows where (looking for sites they'd told me, but that was all I knew) the letter came through from the Essex branch of the Land Army. I was to report on Sunday at 16.00 hours in Epping High Street, from where a lorry would take me and others to Raines Hall in Harlow, where there was to be a hostel established. I would be employed by the local War Agricultural Committee and then hired out to farmers who needed labourers and would pay the Committee for my services. My pay would be 28 shillings a week, and I would need to pay my hostel costs for accommodation and food out of that. I should bring all my Land Army uniform and protective gear against the elements, and just one other change of clothing. I was never to mix my own clothing with the uniform, which had to be worn on all duties and at Sunday services. Within me I could already feel the first stirrings of rebellion, the same emotions that had led to my two school expulsions. I would need to grit my teeth and dampen that rebellious spirit, I knew, if I was to survive the coming months. Unfortunately, I did not manage to do that sufficiently, as you will see.

I made it to Epping Station in quite good time, after catching trains across town and through the suburbs into Essex. But the station was not as near to the High Street as I had supposed it would be, and my case was heavy because I had not exactly followed the WarAg Committee's instructions about what to pack. Some make-up was essential, and I'd never gone anywhere with just one change of clothing. So it was a very large and heavy suitcase that I had to haul up the hill from the station, and I arrived ten minutes late, finding two lorries and nineteen other new Land Army recruits already loaded and waiting for me

"You're late!" one of the drivers said to me sharply. He was a small mean-looking man in shabby clothes, with a burned-out rolled-up cigarette between his lips. He managed to speak without moving the cigarette.

"Yes, I'm sorry. Some idiot thought this was a better place to meet than the station, which would have been much easier. It delayed me getting up here." I should have thought before saying this, but I was exhausted from the walk with my case, and that cigarette dangling from his lips really had distracted me.

"I'm the idiot who thought you should muster here. This has always been the muster point for those serving their country. No-one would see you at the station. Here everyone can see you muster."

I could understand his reasoning, but I was not prepared to give way myself. "Then you could have offered to collect us at the station, and we would have all mustered here on time."

The other women, already seated on their cases on the flat backs of the lorries, were turning to look at our argument. The driver was staring at me as if a woman had never answered him back in his life, and could only splutter his anger. The other driver came from his cab and said, "What's going on? Let's get going."

"This one insulted all of us who've mustered here over the years," his mate answered. "I've a good mind to leave her here to find her own way."

I looked pleadingly at the other driver, who was younger and better dressed than the other one. I had no idea where Raines Hall was, nor how I would get there if I was not transported there with the others. I turned my head slightly and showed him how uncomfortable I felt at that prospect. Fortunately for me, on this occasion my simpering worked, and he told me to get on his lorry instead of the one I was supposed to be on. He even helped me up, though he did comment on the weight of my case. "Heavier than the others," he said in a knowing way, and winked. "Ignore that miserable bastard though. He's always moaning at something."

The journey was bumpy, and the breeze caught all of us trying to hang on to hats or hairbands that threatened to blow away. As we pulled in to Raines Hall I saw that it was a grey, rather forbidding and unadorned building, rectangular in all its doors, windows, chimney breasts and outbuildings. "Looks just like school," one of the Girls said half to herself. I couldn't help agreeing.

We alighted from the lorries with as much dignity as we could and gathered into a kind of line with our bags and cases. A middle-aged woman dressed all in black emerged through the front door with a clipboard in her hand. She looked severely at us, and then I saw the angry driver speaking to her and pointing towards me. She came over to me and spoke angrily. "The driver said you'd insulted the armed services and him when you were late arriving at Epping. What's your name, young woman?"

"Virginia," I answered, "though people generally call me Ginny." One or two of the girls near me giggled at this, but I did not realise why. The woman looked even more crossly at them, and then back at me.

"Don't be so smart with me," she almost snarled. "I mean your surname."

"Beauchamp," I replied, "I'm sorry I didn't understand you wanted that."

The woman was scanning down a list of names on the sheet of paper on her clipboard. "I can't see that name on my list. There's a Beauchamp." She pronounced it as if it were the two original French words.

"Yes, that's me. It's pronounced Beecham."

"Well ,why isn't it spelled that way? Rude to the driver, and now rude to me. You'll need to cut out all that rudeness now." She gave me one last contemptuous look and marched away to the front of our line.

"Blimey," the Girl said who had likened the Hall to a school. "Not just a school but a headmistress as well, eh, Ginny?"

She grinned at me, and I laughed back. "I don't do very well with headmistresses," I said.

She grinned again and held out her hand, and I was grateful to shake it. "I'm Louise Emmers, Ginny. Known as Lewi. Maybe we should room together." I liked the confident way she had introduced herself, so I agreed. As others edged forward to find out a room number, we held back until just we two were left. The Warden, Miss Capthorn, for that was how she introduced herself to us, allocated us the last available room, a small former servants' room up under the eaves. "You'll have to make do there," she said with a bitter smile. "It's small and the walls slope, but you'll be out all day any way. Dinner at 18.30 and breakfast at 07.00 hours in the morning. The lorries will be here to take you to the farms at 08.00. Please be on time, Miss Beauchamp." At least she pronounced it correctly this time.

In the hour before dinner I found out a great deal about Lewi, because she was happy to talk about herself when I asked her questions. She was a pretty young woman, agile and athletic in build but not over-curvaceous. Her hair was brown and she had a little peaches and cream in her complexion. She lived in Waltham Abbey, so she had not moved far in coming to Harlow. She had worked in a shop but had found that dull and repetitive and had thought that an outdoor life doing something more useful might be preferable. She still lived in the small, terraced house where her parents had raised her and her four older brothers. "My mother just kept going until she had a girl," she said. "But can you imagine having four older brothers? More like the four horsemen of the apocalypse," she said with mock horror. From observing friends' families at the two schools I had attended, I understood her thinking. Big brothers were often insufferably superior in attitude, full of themselves, and viewed most friends of their sisters as the necessary objects for fulfilling their not well-concealed desires. "So I spent most of my spare time in the library." And she was very well-read – Dickens, Austen, Hardy, Wells, the Brontes – she reeled them off. And then she started re-enacting some of her favourite scenes for my entertainment. Pip encountering the escaped convict on the Kent marshes; Cathy's spirit snatching at Lockwood from beyond the window pane; Emma getting things wrong again. I had some vague recollections of the stories which I did not know anywhere near as well as Lewi. But she ended the period before dinner by telling me that all four brothers had joined up, and that two had gone to the Far East and two had been rescued from the beach at Dunkirk. Her one sorrow in joining the Land Army was that her parents would for the most part be alone now.

The food at dinner was awful. There is no other word for it. Overcooked cabbage, undercooked potatoes and burned sausages, with a brown liquid masquerading as gravy. I could only eat half my portions, but Lewi, having already eaten all of hers, promptly polished off the reminder of mine. "Comes from having to compete with the four horsemen," she explained, "you never knew if they'd leave you any food at all at the next meal."

I told her how my father had kept delaying our return to England, staying close to the Polish government-in-exile and the dwindling band of ambassadors and others who moved South and finally West when there was no other alternative. I knew he'd been hoping that some word would come via a courier or other means, telling him that she was now following him and where he should meet her. But no message had arrived, not even one telling him she was still alive. And then, to my chagrin, I broke down in full shoulder-shaking sobs, and confessed I thought I would never see her again. I suppose it was talking to another young woman, as opposed to my father and Henri, who both kept their feelings to themselves. Lewi, whom I'd known for barely three hours, held me while I cried, and finally whispered to me, "You will, you will, you know you will. Don't ever stop thinking that." I guessed later that she must have had similar thoughts about her brothers. She certainly knew the right things to say to me.

Next morning I dressed in the shirt, sweater and breeches of my uniform, and pulled the ugly boots over the woollen stockings. I grabbed my hat and hurried down to breakfast – we were late again because I had spent too long putting on make-up and entreating Lewi to wait for me – ate a few spoonfuls of lumpy porridge and a slice of buttered toast, and picked up the cheese rolls and apple that had been prepared for each of us. Lewi and I did make the line-up outside the building at eight, as required by Miss Capthorn, so she could not chide us for that. The same two drivers were there, and while the one scowled at me the other winked and shrugged his shoulders. Miss Capthorn had another list, this time of the requirements of various farmers to whom the drivers would deliver us. "Emmers and Beauchamp," she had taken to putting a particular emphasis on the "ee" of Beecham, as if parodying me, "you're to go to Church Lane Farm near the airfield at North Weald. Farmer says the cabbage field hasn't been hoed all year." I groaned, and Lewi looked at me questioningly. I shook my head and whispered that I would explain later. We found out that Bob, the younger and more pleasant of the drivers, would take us there along with some other Girls who were to be dropped off in places I'd never heard of before: Thornwood, Hastingwood and Coopersale.

"What's wrong with cabbages?" Lewi asked after we had sat down on a tarpaulin that Bob had spread across the floor of the lorry.

"It's not the cabbages, it's the hoeing. It's really hard on the shoulders and back. I'd have preferred almost anything to start with but hoeing."

One of the other girls asked if I'd worked on a farm before, so I told them about my mother's unusual "punishment" of me that summer I'd spent slaving on the farms, and I spent the journey telling them some of the silly mistakes I'd made and their consequences, such as dropping a basketful of eggs, and cutting down growing vegetables which I'd mistaken for weeds, and that passed the time. I was grateful for the sweater I'd put on because the back of the lorry was obviously breezy, but I could see that it was shaping up to be a hot day. The sun was shining brightly in an almost cloudless sky and I checked in the knapsack that Henri had insisted I should pack that I had my metal water bottle – "The British Army seems to think its troops don't need water, Miss Virginia," he had said, "and I dare say the Land Army will be the same." Lewi had laughed when I'd dragged the old khaki-coloured bag out of my case, but she'd stuffed her sandwiches and apple in it gratefully enough, because she didn't have a bag or a water bottle.

Bob dropped us by the side of the road where he'd been instructed to leave us, next to a large field in which cabbages were growing. And alongside the cabbages weeds of every kind were sprouting as well. I pointed them out to Lewi. "I think we're in for a very hard day. I've not hoed anything as bad as that."

After five minutes a farmer drove up on a tractor. He had two hoes tied to the back of his seat. "You the Land Girls?" he asked. I could have been very sarcastic in response, and Lewi guessed that and took my arm to check me, but I simply waved my hands down my uniform to confirm that we were indeed Land Girls, and I said, "Yes, we're ready for your cabbages."

He untied the hoes and ushered us into the field through a gate and said gruffly, "The last two who were here didn't know their arses from their elbows. Let the bull out of its field and caused havoc. I hope you know what you're doing." Lewi looked to me to take the lead.

"I've hoed before," I said, "some years ago, but I think I can still remember what to do."

He pointed to the nearest lines of youngish cabbages, which were visible though starting to be outgrown by some of the weeds. "Show me," he said.

I grabbed one of the hoes and set to work, trying to remain as erect as possible and not to bend over, which I remembered led to awful pain if done for too long. First I scratched out the weeds that were evident on those parts of the furrow that had not been seeded, and then I dragged the hoe's edge across the area beneath the cabbage leaves, taking care to avoid their stems. After that I used the hoe to break the earth up a little and to shape it into a mound between the cabbages. That was how the Polish farm labourers had taught me to hoe. The farmer was surprised. "Why did you do that last bit?" he asked. "I've never seen that done." He was evidently astonished that a Land Girl might know something he didn't.

"The people who taught me said it was so that the growing cabbage could rest on the slope more easily than if you left it flat."

"Well, well," he said. "You seem to know more than the last two. I'll leave you to get on. The lorry will pick you up at five. If I'm not here, lave the hoes near the gate, lying on the ground, ready for tomorrow. Don't take too long for lunch." And with that said, he left on his tractor.

"Lazy bugger," Lewi commented about him. "He obviously hasn't wanted to hoe the field. Nor even to walk down to see us. But I'm glad you know all about this. You can teach me."

I did teach her before we started. I also got some dock leaves from the side of the field and wrapped them around the handles of the hoes. "We'll get blisters," I said, "it's almost certain. But the leaves will stop them from being too bad. Perhaps tomorrow we might find some gloves that we can wear if we're doing this again."

We worked our way from the corner of the field along two furrows, keeping up with each other, and then back again. Lewi found it hard to stand erect and exert the pressure on the hoe, but I kept warning her that she needed to do it correctly. After the first hour the familiar pain between the shoulder blades started to hurt me. I asked Lewi how she was, and she had the same pain. It came from using our arms and shoulders in ways that were unfamiliar and very repetitive, and I knew that it was going to hurt until our muscles had grown used to the work. I just encouraged Lewi to keep going, but she said that she needed to go to the toilet. "Where is it?" she asked.

"Back at the farmhouse, I suppose, but I don't know where that is."

"But I really need to go. I had two mugs of tea at breakfast, and now they're raring to leave me again."

In Poland, I recalled, there were no toilets anywhere near the fields. Many of the farms still had a completely separate building housing a water closet which was the only toilet available, even in the deepest snow. The farmers, their wives and children, and the labourers, had all simply urinated or defecated on the fields, crouching down if necessary. I told Lewi this, and she was momentarily annoyed and flustered, protesting at the indignity of it. But then she relented and accepted the inevitable. "I don't suppose you brought any of that toilet paper with you?"

"You mean the paper you ridiculed me for having last night?" I joked. She acknowledged the point but put her hands together as if in prayer. "There's some in the knapsack, over at the edge of the field. So poor Lewi was the first of us to have to pee in the field, pulling her breeches and underwear down and crouching embarrassedly by the hedge and between the rows of cabbages. But before the day was over we had both got used to it, and all we did was check that no-one was passing on the road or could otherwise see us.

It was a hot day, and the sun never found a cloud to hide behind. We kept our hats on, even though the rims became sweat-soaked, but we tried to get some air on our legs by pulling the breeches up as if they were shorts and pulling our socks down. We stopped working at midday and found what little shade we could, and sat there to eat our food and drink the water. When it came to standing up and returning to work, neither of us could do so easily. "I didn't know I had muscles there," Lewi said, pointing down the centre of her back. "But I do now."

From time to time during the morning we were disturbed by the take-off or landing of one of the fighters at the nearby airfield. They did not seem to be headed off for an aerial battle anywhere but seemed rather just to circle the general area once or twice and then land again. The afternoon was quiet, and we had just reached the end of one of the rows and were standing by the hedge next to the road, when an open car carrying four young men pulled up. "Hello Land Girls," one of the four shouted as he peered over the hedge. "How are you?"

Lewi answered first, returning their greeting and asking who they were. "Pilots from the airfield," another one answered. "Searching out the local sights, and you two are one of the more pleasant ones." I doubted that. We by that time were looking decidedly unkempt, hot and sweaty. I wouldn't bother with make-up tomorrow, I had resolved to myself, since I thought it had run and merged with my sweat into an unsightly mess. Nonetheless it was intended as a slightly flirtatious compliment, and we were probably both grateful for that. We went nearer and talked to them over the hedge. The two who had already spoken explained that they had been transferred to Essex after they'd been involved in the hundreds of sorties flown over Dunkirk and its surrounding lands and beaches to protect the Expeditionary Force. Their planes were being mended and serviced in anticipation of a coming renewal of combat, what Churchill had called the Battle for Britain. So they had some free time and were filling it up as best they could. They suggested we could join them that evening and bring a couple of friends if we wanted. I wasn't sure this was a good idea, and Lewi looked similarly doubtful. Two of the pilots had stayed silent to this point, but one of them suddenly burst out, "Ginny, Ginny Beauchamp. That's you, isn't it? Of all the people, in all the places, you're here in a cabbage field?"

I looked closer. I recognised the man. He was Roger Madesmith, who had been on the edge of the group I had hung around with in 1938 when I was in London for a few weeks. And when I'd had that incident with the police and the magistrates! "And I recognise you. I haven't seen you for a couple of years, Roger, but you've not changed much, except in becoming a pilot." I pointed at the clothes he was wearing, half of which looked like a pilot's uniform.

Roger insisted on introducing all of the others. The other silent one was Piotr, a Pole, Roger said. I greeted him in Polish, and he looked first surprised, and then pleased. He greeted me back, and we started a conversation in Polish that led us aside from the other three pilots and Lewi, who chatted but also watched us. He was darkly handsome, black-haired and blue-eyed. He told me that he came from a town near Poznan but had been based with a fighter unit near the border with Germany when the attack came. He had fought against the Luftwaffe, and gradually they had retreated to bases further east and south, until finally he and others had fled with their planes and tried to reach Serbia. But the Hungarians had forced their planes down and denied them fuel, so they had to leave the planes behind, and journey on by foot and by begging lifts, following much the same route that my father and I had taken. Arriving in England he had persuaded the British authorities to let him fly with the RAF, by proving that his English was good, but they were only convinced when they saw him fly and he told them of his battle experience. He had not been allowed to fly over Dunkirk but had now been cleared to fly in the battle that they were all anticipating. Then he asked more about me, and I explained as briefly as I could my life story. He nodded and smiled as he understood it, obviously enjoying speaking his native tongue again. Then I realised how long we'd been chatting and said to Lewi that we'd better resume work or the farmer would be complaining about us.

"Hang on one minute, though," Roger said, and made me walk a little away from the others. "You haven't said if you're going to come out with us tonight."

"I don't think we should tonight. We've only just arrived and we're dog-tired."

"But Piotr would like it. He's usually just silent and pretty miserable, but now he's found you he's been smiling and gabbling away."

"Look, make it Friday or Saturday and we'll do it." I hoped Lewi would back me up. "And I'll try to get two more of the Girls to make up a… an… an eightsome." We both laughed. We agreed that the pilots would pick us up at Raines Hall at six- thirty in the evening on Saturday, and we'd visit a couple of pubs.

When they'd gone I told Lewi what I'd agreed. She was nervous about it, asking me if it would be alright, and if she could trust these pilots. I answered positively, though I really should have had my fingers crossed. We worked on, though we became hot, thirsty and full of ache. Just before five o'clock the farmer turned up, again driving his tractor. He looked at what we'd done, and then said, "Thanks very much, ladies. I would not have expected that two Land

Girls would be able to do what you have managed. I'm very grateful, especially when the first hoeing was never done after the men left for the army. And I couldn't do it because after a lifetime of doing this work, I can't lift my arms even to shoulder height." Lewi and I looked at one another, no doubt both feeling guilty over our earlier view of his laziness. "Yes, I'll ask for you to come back tomorrow." We had to supress our groans – we'd done too well. It might have been better for us if we'd cut down the cabbages and left the weeds standing tall!

Soon after that Bob pulled up his lorry by the gate to the field, and the farmer gave Bob a message for our warden. We could hardly climb up at the tail of the vehicle, and Bob had to push us up in an undignified way, no doubt enjoying grabbing our behinds in the process, so that we could slump on the floor. The other Girls looked at us in surprise – none of them, it seemed, had worked as hard as we had. And our state of mind was not improved when we reached Raines Hall. All the hot water had been used up by the Girls returning before us on the other lorry. We couldn't even have a bath, though Lewi briefly considered running one with just cold water. We ate our dinner in near silence and sneaked off for an early night and a long sleep, though the aches and pains in our backs and limbs made that hard to achieve.

CHAPTER 4
JUNE 25TH-29TH 1940

The Warden surprised us at breakfast by clapping her hands for silence and then in front of all the others congratulating Lewi and me because our farmer had sent his particular thanks to us for our day's work. She hoped that this would inspire everyone to understand how we were needed and appreciated. I surprised myself by eating all the porridge, though I did not match Lewi by drinking two mugs of tea. There were only so many times in one day I wanted to crouch down in a cabbage field with my knickers around my ankles. The weather was overcast, and Lewi and I had been warned the day before what that might mean. If it was raining when we arrived for work, the farmer had to find us indoor work instead of in the fields, but if it started raining after we started work, we had to carry on despite the rain. We had brought our mackintoshes, therefore, and our rubber boots, and I found myself hoping that it would rain on us as we crouched on the back of our lorry. But the rain held off until we were half an hour into our day's work, and hoeing in a mackintosh and rubber boots was not easy. The clay beneath our feet became slippery, and the hoe skidded across it rather than biting into it. We were soaked by the time the farmer turned up around midday to tell us that his wife had insisted he bring us to the farmhouse, and we climbed gratefully up on the tractor, hanging on to its guard rails. His wife allowed us into her kitchen to dry out and eat our lunch, and then the farmer found us some work cleaning and tidying up in the various outhouses that were near the farmhouse itself.

Working together now, Lewi and I had more time to talk. She started by telling me how our work resembled that of the agricultural workers in the various novels of Thomas Hardy that she had read. She compared me to Bathsheba in "Far from the Madding Crowd" and then she re-enacted Sergeant Troy's wooing of her. She made me laugh, which I realised I hadn't done very much in a long time. But then she asked me more seriously about the pilots who had asked us to go out with them. "I know I should know a lot about boys and men, having four older brothers, but the truth is they always seemed to stand in the way of my meeting any other boys. Will everything be alright? I've heard some people say that pilots are a bit reckless and want girls to come along with them for just one thing. And I've no experience to tell me what to do."

"Lewi," I said, "I think it's true that these men know more about fear and death than we do. They've experienced both, but all they want is to be happy in some company for a few hours. One of them may want to kiss you, perhaps, but that too would probably just be for the sake of holding someone else close. If one wanted you just for sex, they wouldn't be going out in… what did I call it, an eightsome. But if one of them does try it on, do what my mother advised me the first time she let me go out in a group of women and men."

"What was that?"

"She told me that if I felt a man's hand on my knee, or any higher, I should immediately say to him that it's my time of the month, sorry. And do you know, it works. That hand will disappear faster than if you'd said there was a snake lurking up your skirt."

Lewi gave me a look that showed her questioning whether I was being serious or not. "No really, "I said, "it does work. But I don't think you'll need that strategy on Saturday night. Of more concern will be keeping them sober enough to drive us home safely."

It was dry for the remainder of the week, which meant that we continued with our hoeing. In a shed at Raines Hall we had managed to find some old gardening gloves that we could use, but we still had painful blisters on our hands. Our shoulders and arms ached, and we were exhausted by the end of our work on Saturday. It would have been better if we had simply collapsed on our beds and fallen asleep, but I had found two of the other Girls who would come out with us, and so we quickly prepared ourselves for the outing. We also skipped dinner, which with hindsight was foolish, because we were going out drinking alcohol on empty stomachs. And we trusted the pilots to bring us back to Raines Hall in good time. Foolish, foolish, foolish! Wasn't that how the virgins were described in the Bible?

The pilots had from somewhere borrowed another car, so all eight of us set off in convoy. Roger had pushed me into the back of the first car with Piotr, and Lewi had taken the spare front seat. The other four were all in the other car. Roger said that he'd arranged for us to visit two local pubs that he'd been told were good, and he led the way to the first, which was about three miles away. Piotr chatted to me in Polish, asking me how the week had gone. I complained about all my aches and blisters, and about getting soaked when it rained. I said that we'd still seen planes taking off and landing, but that I hadn't seen any mass take-offs of the kind that they must have had for their forays over France. He agreed, though he said that they were really forbidden to talk of operational matters, but that they were still preparing for what everyone expected. I thought then of my father, busy preparing sites and factories where more planes could be built, no doubt to replace those which they expected to be shot down by the Luftwaffe. And the Germans would no doubt also be preparing, taking over airfields in France, Belgium and Holland, so that they could attack us from the air. And I realised fully, which I had not done before, how many of the young pilots like Piotr and Roger and their two friends would die or be seriously injured in the coming battle. I shuddered, and Piotr noticed. I think he thought I was cold in the draught caused by sitting in an open car. He put his arm around me and held me tightly towards him. I didn't object. How could I, given what I had just realised?

We did visit two pubs and had probably too much to drink. One of the Girls, Ellen, had brought a squeezebox with her, and she played it so that we could dance. The publicans and the locals did not object, indeed they bought the pilots several rounds and joined in the dancing. No doubt they had had similar thoughts to those which had struck me in the car as I sat next to Piotr. Next week, next month, these young men might be dead, or lying shattered or burned in a hospital bed. But for now they were our main protection from the evil that had swept across Europe, and if they wanted to enjoy themselves no-one was going to stop them. I danced with each of the pilots, with Roger regaling me with stories of our mutual friends and acquaintances. Some had joined up, others were in the course of joining, and some had fled to America. One or two were already dead, killed in defending France or lost at sea. I suppose it was becoming normal to know of people in Britain whom the war had taken. We were just catching up with other countries that had already experienced this loss.

Piotr held me more closely as we danced, and whispered in my ear how much he was enjoying speaking Polish and thinking of his homeland while I was with him. He said that the men at the airfield tried to show their confidence and cheerfulness, but that inside everyone was thinking about what was likely to happen soon. He said that he had held similar fears during the previous autumn, while fleeing from the advancing Germans, but that he no longer had such thoughts. If something was to happen to him, so be it, he claimed. But he so wanted to fight back against those who had taken his country – which he corrected to our country. Shortly after that, he asked me to walk in the garden of the pub, and as we walked he asked if he could hold me. I agreed, and we embraced closely. He asked then if he could kiss me, and again I said yes, even allowing him to cup my breast with his hand as he did so. It was a passionate kiss, but something was missing, either on my part or his. We both had a sense of how transitory our lives were, I think, and how we were just taking some comfort from each other as we could that evening. But it could not go further. I was determined on my commitment to avoiding pregnancy, and he, I think, simply felt that he could not go further without compromising either himself or me, when most of his thoughts were focussed on his immediate future, which did not involve me. So we kissed for a long time, and then broke off as I realised how late we were out, when Raines Hall would be shut to us at ten o'clock.

It must have taken me ten minutes just to get the other seven to finish their drinks and get in the cars. Herding cats would definitely have been easier. But that was not the cause of our difficulties. I had not thought about the fact that the night would grow dark, the men could not use the cars' headlights, and every road sign had been removed from the corners and crossroads where one would need to make decisions about the next part of our route home. To me, and I fear to all the others, every field, hamlet, wood or part of the wider Epping Forest looked similar in the darkness to the ones we had passed ten minutes previously. There were no pedestrians at this time of the night out in the countryside, so no-one from whom we could beg directions. When we seemed to be passing the same small village green for the third time I asked Roger if we were lost. "Not at all," he answered, "just a little unsure of our directions. If I was a thousand feet up in the air, I'd know which way to go."

"That's because you'd have a compass," Piotr muttered. He fumbled in his pockets and produced a small pocket compass. "Would this help?" he asked.

"Be prepared, eh?" Roger said in jest, but he did nonetheless look closely at it. "I think we were to the south-east of Raines Hall at that pub. Let's see if going north-west helps us." He handed Lewi the compass, but she looked blankly at him, so he turned and gave it to Piotr instead. "Keep us going north-west, would you. And don't let Ginny distract you."

I let the insulting joke pass. There was no point having a row when we were obviously in difficulty. Roger set off again, the other car still following behind, and Piotr gave Roger the direction at every junction we came to. After several miles of travelling like this, Lewi suddenly said, "Hang on, I think I recognise that church. We passed it every day last week." She tried to remember our route as she had seen it from the back of the lorry, and we did finally find our way to Raines Hall.

I looked at the watch on Piotr's wrist. "Oh God," I groaned, "eleven o'clock. Now we're for it."

"Rubbish!" Roger exclaimed, and before I could stop him he had gone to the front door of the Hall and hammered on the knocker several times. The sound was like gunshot in the dark, and it reverberated for several seconds after each loud rap. "What can they do to you?" he asked, looking back at us as we clambered out of the vehicles. "You were only enjoying yourselves with some of His Majesty's servicemen."

"That's just why they might discipline us," one of the Girls said. I sympathised with Roger, but I did think that he might have hesitated before rousing all the inhabitants of the Hall. As someone experienced in the arts of escaping and re-entering supposedly closed institutions, my two boarding schools for example, I knew that what you didn't do was draw your guards' and monitors' attention to you as you effected the re-entry. Better just to get someone sleeping in one of the ground floor bedrooms to open the window to let you sneak in. Or to go round the back and see if every door really was firmly locked and bolted on the inside. At worst, sleep in an outhouse and sneak in quietly in the morning, trying to avoid being noticed. Unfortunately for us, it was Miss Capthorn who was roused by Roger's knocking at the front door, and she was dressed in a dressing-gown and a face of ire. She surveyed the scene with a truly dismal look. Medusa herself could not have turned her victims to stone more quickly. Roger was frozen on the doorstep in the porch. We Girls were shame-facedly looking at the ground to avoid seeing her. And the other three pilots had stopped talking and were looking on with the fascination of movie-goers at a horror film.

Finally Miss Capthorn spoke. "Go to your rooms, ladies. We'll deal with this matter in the morning."

So we filed past our Warden, muttering our apologies. Roger didn't help by regaining his confidence and saying, "Goodnight, ladies. Goodnight sweet ladies, goodnight, goodnight." I don't think Miss Capthorn had read either "The Waste Land" or "Hamlet", so she must have thought he was just mocking her.

I was upset by the time we got to our room. I suppose my history of rebellion and punishment meant that I knew when some vindictive sanction was about to be applied. Lewi was not so aware, probably because she had not my previous experience nor my sense of foreboding. "What can she do?" she asked. "They need us more than we need them."

I explained that my record of expulsion and brushing with the law had meant that I felt I was under a kind of probation, and that I was afraid that I might be dismissed. Lewi was kind in her rejection of that possibility. "Ginny," she said, "you knew more than the farmer who was supposed to tell us what to do. They wouldn't dismiss you. Now tell me about Piotr!" This was said with a knowing tone. I tried to protest my innocence, but Lewi was adamant. "I saw you snogging him in the pub garden. We all did, I think. What's between you?"

"What does 'snogging' mean?" I asked. "I've never heard the word before."

"You know what it means. It means you were sharing a full-on kiss." Lewi laughed. "You know, tongues and all. Even I know that, though the four horsemen stopped me ever snogging anyone."

"I've never heard the word before. Yes we were kissing, though our tongues weren't as involved as you might think."

"Not just tongues, Ginny. I thought you might need that word of advice from your mother any moment there. You were saved by the bell. It was time to come back."

"No I didn't need my mother's advice. He was too… too…too gentlemanly for that."

"Methinks you do protest too much. That's Shakespeare you know." I didn't, but something inside me suggested that there was a word of truth in Lewi's accusations. I did feel something for Piotr that was not just sympathy with his loneliness as a Polish pilot in the RAF. But attack is the best means of defence, and I suggested to Lewi that she hadn't got on so badly with Roger, and that she was obviously enjoying being away from the malign control of her brothers. She laughed and whispered something about people living in glass houses before starting to undress and put her nightwear on. I was slower to do this, still feeling that yet again I had transgressed, crossed a line that I should have recognised and halted at, and would suffer the consequences next day.

And I did! Suffer the consequences, that is. Next morning at the end of breakfast Miss Capthorn said that she wanted to see the four of us in her office. By now the other Girls knew what had happened, and there was some sympathising with us, while others watched with interest and not a little delight in our predicament. It had been much the same both times I was expelled, I recalled.

We went in one by one. I didn't like that. It meant that as I was last, I didn't know what the others had said, not least because they were let out of another door than the one I was standing outside, and told to go to their rooms for the remainder of the day. When I was called in, I was surprised to find another woman with Miss Capthorn. She was introduced as Lady Wakeham, who was in charge of the Land Army for the whole district. She spoke bluntly and without allowing me to interject. "Miss Beauchamp, I am most disappointed by your behaviour, especially when I'm told that your father is conducting urgent business on behalf of the government. I thought that you would make a good recruit to the Land Army, because you had told them in recruitment that you wanted to impress by your contribution. Instead you've done one thing wrong after another. You've been late. You've been rude. And now it seems you've been fraternising with pilots from North Weald, who surely have more urgent and pressing matters to worry about than you. And you were late back and drunk last night."

"It is my fault," I said in as apologetic a tone as I could. "I knew one of the pilots and he asked me to get the others to come out with them. But we were only enjoying their company. I was not drunk." I had my fingers crossed, of course.

"Huh," Lady Wakeham said to Miss Capthorn. "I see what you mean."

I knew that I shouldn't respond, and I certainly know now that I shouldn't have, but that was just a red rag waved at me. "Yes, Lady Wakeham. Enjoying their company, just as they were enjoying ours. For goodness sake, do you not understand that next week, next month, next year, they could all be dead. They're living with that knowledge every day. So they just wanted a little distraction, a little pleasure, that's all. But in the dark, and without signposts, we got lost. That's why we were late. I take full responsibility for it."

"I think you do bear most of the responsibility, Miss Beauchamp. And you've done enough in a week to warrant dismissal from the Army. Do you really think that Herr Hitler is going to send all his pilots and planes to fight against ours? These men will all still be alive and well in a year's time. Hitler has got France and the Low Countries. That's all Germany has ever wanted. He won't want to lose his Luftwaffe over England."

"That's not what Churchill thinks, is it?" I countered. I had heard of people who thought like this Lady Wakeham, but I hadn't thought that anyone in a position of authority could be so blind to the inevitable attack that was coming.

"What do you know of such matters, Miss Beauchamp? Any way, they are not for us. As I say, you really warrant dismissal, but there is one thing standing in your good stead. The farmer you've worked for couldn't have a higher opinion of you. He told Miss Capthorn that, but he also wrote to the WarAg Committee saying that taking you on was the best thing he'd done in years. Why, when you can do such good work, do you insist on being so rude, and late, and troublesome?"

I couldn't answer really. It was roughly what my two headmistresses had said at similar points in my past. I shrugged, to signal that I really didn't know why these things happened to me. I think my shrug was seen as another example of my rudeness.

"I've decided to transfer you to Houblions Hill Farm. The farmer there is under pressure and there are already two Land Girls working there. Go and pack your things and I will see if I can get some transport. And remember, Miss Beauchamp, this is the last warning I will give you. Next time I will dismiss you."

I did try to interject, to argue that it was unfair to separate me from some new friends that I had made – I was thinking particularly of Lewi – and that I could do a good job in helping the other Girls who were not as familiar with farming as I was. I had shown how well I could do that already. But it was like arguing with my old headmistresses. Her mind was made up before she spoke to me. There was no room for change. I left the room and trudged upstairs to the room I shared with Lewi. She was lying on her bed but jumped up as I entered. "I'm confined to the premises for two weeks," she said angrily. "What about you?"

"Sent packing to another farm and billet, Lewi," I said in reply. "Houblions Hill, I think she called it. And she gave me a last warning. I only just missed being dismissed. I tried arguing, but it was no use."

"I'll go and see her," Lewi offered. "That's so unfair on you. And on me. I was just getting to know you, and I thought I'd found a friend." She made to go, but I held her back.

"No, Lewi. That won't work. It will just get you into worse difficulty with them. You are right about us being friends, though. I'll give you my address, both at the farm and in town, and perhaps you'd give me your parents' address so that I can contact you if you're not here."

I packed quickly, just throwing my things into the case rather than folding them or rolling them carefully as my mother had always insisted I should. I wrote down my addresses, and took the paper on which Lewi had written hers, and I hugged her by way of a farewell, though I sensed that she was still angry at Lady Wakeham's snap judgements. I dragged my suitcase down the two flights of stairs, and to the front door. A few of the Girls were sitting on the front lawn chatting, and they asked me what was happening. I explained my punishment and they sympathised with me, and said that they would look out for Lewi in the coming days and make sure the others were talking to her and socialising with her as well. One complained of Miss Capthorn in similar terms to the remark Lewi had made when we arrived. "It's just like being in flaming school, isn't it? We can be trusted to go and do our work labouring on the farms, but not to make our own decisions about our own time." Lewi opened the window of the room we had shared and waved to me as I left.

CHAPTER 5
JUNE 30ᵀᴴ 1940

I was taken by car to the farm where I was next to work. We went into and out of Epping, and I noted that I would not be very far from the railway that would allow me to travel into London. I would also still not be very far from North Weald airfield, and I wondered how Roger and Piotr would react to news of my removal. I didn't suppose it would matter much to them. They had much more important things to think about, as Lady Wakeham had at least acknowledged.

Houblions Hill Farm was a large farm extending eastward from the road that gave it its name. The farmhouse was by the road, and was a three storey Georgian building, which had perhaps been at the centre of a larger estate that had been broken up. There was a series of outbuildings behind the main house, and a tall barn set to one side. I guessed that the fields that we had passed as we approached were part of the farm. I had seen cattle in one of the fields, and so thought that the work was likely to involve rising early if milking was involved. But some of the other fields clearly had crops that were growing towards a harvest.

The car left me by the road so I walked along the short drive to the house and knocked at the front door. A white-haired woman answered, drying her hands on the apron. From inside the house the smell of cooking wafted through the open door. The woman seemed at first not to recognise who I was, perhaps because I was not wearing my uniform. "Yes?" she asked.

"I'm Virginia Beauchamp," I said in reply. "I'm from the Land Army. I've been transferred here from Harlow. They said you were short of people."

"Oh, you've arrived," she said, a little brusquely I thought. "Let's hope you're better than those we've been left with." That seemed a particularly strange remark, and I was nonplussed. She seemed to realise that her response was not clear to me, and said, "Go around the back of the house and find the black door. Your quarters are there, and I think one other Girl is there at the moment. She'll tell you what to do. I'm busy cooking and can't stop now." And with that said, she shut the door in my face. I'd been greeted in some strange ways in my life before, but perhaps never as strangely as that.

I trudged around the house and quickly surveyed the yard that was behind it. The barn to my right was imposing. It had two large wooden doors in a flint and brick wall, and high above the doors was a large opening with a winch and pulley above it. A rope looped into the barn. The upper storey was obviously used to store tools, equipment, hay or straw that would need winching down before use. The lower storey was the dairy, and there were some stalls that were empty. The other outbuildings were squat and shabby, with low roofs that had lost the odd tile here and there. In the middle of the outbuildings was one with a black door, so I crossed the yard to it and knocked with my knuckles on the wood. There was no answer so I tried the door handle and it turned and the door opened rather stiffly and slowly. I called hello into the room that I saw before me, a small sitting room I suppose you'd call it, with two old armchairs, and a gas ring in one corner with some basic cooking utensils. Beyond the room were two doors, and at that moment a young woman opened one and came through the doorway. I again said hello, and this time she noticed me.

"Hello," she said. "You must be the replacement for Mandy."

"I didn't know I was replacing anybody," I answered.

She looked at me. She was not just pretty, she was beautiful —a slender face and figure, shining blue eyes, auburn hair brushed and combed around her face. I always hoped I was passable in the beauty stakes, and Lewi had undoubtedly been what people would call pretty, but this Girl exceeded us both. "I'm Anna," she said in a neutral tone. "They told me they were sending another Girl to replace Mandy."

"I'm Virginia, but people mostly call me Ginny. They transferred me from Harlow and said that the farmer here was under pressure."

"Almost all the men joined up. Only his son Charlie is left to help, and he's talking of joining up even though his parents don't want him to. And the government and War Ag are making him change from dairy to crops, so he's got to plough up lots of fields and reduce the size of the herd. He's not at all happy about it and grumbles all the time. And at the moment he and Susan, his wife, are not very happy with me either." I thought she was going to elucidate this remark, which might also have explained the cryptic welcome the farmer's wife had given me, but she didn't. We stood looking at one another awkwardly for a few moments. Then she showed me the shared room in which I was to sleep. It lay beyond the living room and had a window looking out over the fields. The two beds, the bedding and the wardrobe were all very basic. I said that I would unpack, and Anna offered me a cup of tea, which I was grateful for. When I had finished stuffing my clothes and the Army uniform into the lowest drawer of the wardrobe, I sat down in the front room and drank the tea. Anna looked at me quietly, as if assessing me.

I felt awkward being studied in that way and asked some questions about the arrangements for our work. Anna told me that we had to bring the cows in from the fields at six in the morning, and then guide them four at a time into the milking parlour, and again in the late afternoon. In fact, it was our turn to do this today, Sunday being a day when other work was not done but the milking still had to be arranged. There were four milking machines, something which I had not seen in Poland on the farms where I had worked. These were quick and efficient in producing the milk, and the cows were for the most part responsive, she said. On a normal day, once we had returned all the cows to the fields, we could have our breakfast. Then we had to do other jobs around the farm, including cleaning the outbuildings and bringing down hay and straw from the upper floor of the barn, checking the fencing around the fields used by the cattle, digging out ditches that had become blocked, hoeing the fields in which crops were growing, watering crops where that was possible – Anna explained that there was no water supply for some of the fields – and generally labouring until four in the afternoon, when we would repeat the morning milking. Sometimes the farmer might be helping with the work, and his son Charlie would also work with us. There was a third Land Girl called Katherine. Anna said nothing more, and again we looked at one another, awkward because of the unexpected and unexplained silence.

To fill the silence, I asked about the arrangements for eating, and for our ablutions. I'd seen a small w.c. off the main room, but there did not seem to be a bath. Anna said that Susan would give us breakfast and make us a lunch that we could eat in the fields. She also said that we could have dinner in the farmhouse, but then she said that this had become awkward for her, and that in recent days she had collected her dinner and brought it back to the room in which we were sitting. Again, I thought she might explain this further, but nothing was forthcoming. We were allowed the use of the bathroom in the farmhouse twice a week, but otherwise had to wash in the small room with the water closet. We were charged fifteen shillings a week for this board and lodging. I might normally have been outraged to lose over half my wages for such provision, but I suppose nothing about the Land Army surprised me now, and a farmer making profit at our expense no longer angered me as much as it might have done just two weeks previously.

"So why did the last Girl, Mandy, leave?" I asked, wondering if this might be the route to clarification of the cause of the unhappiness that was obviously in the air.

"She got fed up of all the rows," Anna answered, but again revealed nothing more.

"Why were there rows?" I asked, becoming a little concerned about my new posting. I knew myself too well. If someone started rowing with me, I would probably row back. And then where would I be?

"Because of me," Anna said in a dispirited voice, and she got up from her chair and walked into the toilet, shutting and bolting the door behind her.

I was nonplussed. How could this beautiful, quietly-spoken young woman cause rows sufficient to force another Land Girl to leave her posting? As I was pondering this mystery there was a loud knock on the door. I opened it and Susan, the farmer's wife who had answered the door of the farmhouse, was standing there, her apron still around her waist. She spoke to me quite sharply, "I'm serving the men's dinner in five minutes. You'd be better to come over in half an hour. I'll keep a plate warm for you." And with that she turned on her heel.

"What about Anna?" I called at her departing back. She half-turned and told me in no uncertain terms that she did not know nor care if Anna wanted any dinner, and then hurried back across the yard.

I sat and waited for Anna to emerge, which she did, after around ten minutes. She looked upset, but I still needed some explanation of the tension and bitterness that I had encountered since I arrived. "Was that Susan you were talking to?" Anna asked me.

"Yes. She told me to come and get some dinner in half an hour. And that you might or might not want dinner. What's going on here? Because I'm a bit afraid of putting my foot in it, if I don't know what's making people unhappy." I didn't say anything about why I was especially anxious.

Anna sat down in the other chair and looked sadly at me. She was obviously wondering whether or not to tell me. Finally she dropped her shoulders a little and sighed. "You'd find out soon enough, I suppose. It's to do with Charlie, the farmer's son. He's fallen for me, and his parents don't like it. But I like him as well, and I don't just want to be forced by his parents to give him up. The whole situation is fraught, and they tried to get the Land Army to take me away, but the WarAg people said if they did that they wouldn't replace me at all, which the farm couldn't cope with. So there is a lot of conflict about me. Oh, and

Katherine, the other Girl, fancied her chances with Charlie before I arrived, and now she resents that he's after me, not her."

"But why," I asked, not really understanding what the farmer's objections could be, "are they so opposed to you?"

"Oh, they had big ideas about where the farm was headed before the war broke out. You must have seen the outside of the house, how grand it is. They wanted Charlie to fall for another farmer's daughter, or for someone who would inherit money, so that they could build the farm up. "Take it back to its grand old days." That's what he says about it. But I'm just a shop girl who wanted to do something for the war effort, and my parents don't have the money to buy land and other farm buildings. But I think Charlie really likes me. I don't know what will happen now."

Anna lapsed into silence. I mused about the situation I had been sent into. It certainly seemed full of conflict, but at least on this occasion I was not the cause. I thought that my best plan would be to keep my head down and get on with the work and try to establish the best relations I could with every participant in this domestic drama. So when I went across the yard to get my lunch, I reminded myself of that plan before I knocked at the back door.

Susan, the farmer's wife, greeted me more warmly, though she did seem to check first that I was alone. She sat me down in the kitchen and served up a good roast meal. Because of rationing, one only rarely got a good meal at that time, and I was very grateful for it. "The farmers around here share some of the produce before it goes off for sale in the market," Susan explained, "so at least for the moment we've still been able to eat quite well. Do you have any experience of farms, Miss Beauchamp?"

"Please call me Ginny. It's what I'm used to. As for farming, I did work on some farms in Poland, so I know the rudiments, but I've already heard that you've got machines that I've never seen nor used before. I will have to learn." I started to eat the food, but Susan insisted on questioning me further about my background, my family, and why I was working as a Land Girl. I didn't tell her about failing the medical examination but stuck to the safer lie that I wanted to work outdoors, and I avoided saying anything explicit about my family. She did mention the conflicts that they had been experiencing, but only obliquely. "There's been some unhappiness here around you Land Girls," she stated, "but I hope you will try to fit in and not get involved in any of that." I did not respond, but finished my meal and thanked her. Making my excuses that I had to get ready for the milking, I went back to see how Anna was and what we had to do before the milking. She said that she had cleaned and prepared the dairy after milking that morning, and that all we would need to do was to gather the cows. That should be fine because the grass was very rich so they were producing so much milk that they wanted their udders emptied. And so it proved. I changed into my uniform, and when at four o'clock Anna started to open the gates of the field the herd started to move towards us. They walked steadily through the gate and into the holding paddock, where some nudged forward to be milked first.

I was intrigued to see the milking machines at work. They had suction pads that fixed on the cow's udders, and when the motor started they drew the milk out into a collecting pail. It was fairly straightforward to fix the machine in place. A kind of belt or girdle had to be fixed to the cow first, and I was reminded that the cattle could unexpectedly kick out, so it was best to approach the task from the side and not from the rear. Each full pail was transferred to the churns that stood to one side of the dairy. From there they would need to be transferred for collection by the lorry that collected milk from all the local farms. The farm had four sets of these machines, called surges, and they must have cost a pretty penny because they were imported from America. Anna was obviously repeating what she had been told, either by the farmer or by his son. If they were expensive, I could understand why the farmer was unhappy to have to reduce the number of dairy cattle he kept. His profits would be reduced. Compared with milking by hand, which I had done in Poland, and which left your fingers cramped and your whole hand aching with the hours of repetitive squeezing, these machines were a delight.

Part-way through our work Robert, the farmer himself, looked in. He was a large man, balding and red-faced, and he watched us without saying anything. Anna led four cows out after they had given their milk, and in her absence he spoke to me. "You're alright, are you?" he asked. "Someone's explained what you're to do, clearly, and Susan said you'd done some farm work before."

I nodded and went out to get the next four cows in from the holding paddock. When I came back he and Anna were in a loud conversation. "I'm simply saying," I heard him say, "that it's best if you two keep apart from one another." And without looking back at me, he stumped off. Anna raised her eyebrows at me, as if to say that's what she had to put up with. But no sooner had the father disappeared into the farmhouse than the son appeared at the other door to the dairy. Charlie was tall and well-built, and he looked cheerfully towards Anna. She saw him immediately and took his arm and led him away, no doubt to tell him what his father had just said to her. I simply got on with the task in hand, still milking the final set of four cows, and topping up the churns that were now almost full. When the cows had been milked, I detached them from the machines and led them out to the field to join the herd. I returned to the dairy and started to clear up and clean all the equipment. Then I swept the floor, and used a wheelbarrow to put the used and soiled straw on a compost heap that was behind the barn. Then, as Anna had indicated we would have to do, I started to hose down the floor. All this time Anna was outside somewhere with Charlie, but I didn't mind that particularly. I was grateful to have joined a farm where they had milking machines, knowing what the alternative was like.

Finally Anna returned with Charlie, who was pushing a small cart. He loaded the churns on the cart and said to me, "Ginny, I think you're called. Come and help push and I'll show you where the churns go." We pushed the cart around the side of the farmhouse and along the driveway to the road. Charlie stopped and lifted the churns from the cart and set them down by the roadside. "They'll be collected quite soon and taken to the main dairy for pasteurisation and bottling," he said, "and the next set of churns will be left here. Then you bring those ones in either tonight or tomorrow morning."

Once we had returned to the dairy, he and Anna walked off in the direction of the fields, and I was left to my own devices. I could see that this placement was not going to be as sociable as Raines Hall. Anna was more concerned about Charlie than me, not surprisingly if they were walking out together. I was missing Lewi and her good humour already. As I walked back to our rooms, two RAF fighters flew low over the farm. I wondered if either of them was piloted by Piotr, and then I wondered why I was wondering that.

Later in the evening the third Girl returned after her day off. Katherine was a little older than I or Anna, and tall with curly hair. She had red cheeks and her skin was bronzed by the sun in which she had been working for some months. I could see why Charlie might prefer Anna to walk out with. She would catch people's eyes as soon as they saw her, whereas Katherine by comparison was rather plain. Katherine said little to me before going to the other bedroom, a small single room which I saw briefly before she shut the door.

CHAPTER 6
JULY 8TH-14TH 1940

It was an unusual place and climate in which to work. There was conflict between Charlie and his parents over Anna, and conflict between the parents and Anna over Charlie, and conflict between Anna and Katherine, because Katherine claimed that Charlie had fancied her before Anna arrived, and now wouldn't give her the time of day, as she put it. She also claimed that Charlie's parents favoured her because her father was a bank manager, quite senior she claimed, and that Charlie's parents believed she would bring the necessary money and clout to a marriage to improve the prospect of increasing the farm's size and profits. Robert, the farmer, seemed to think that Hitler had declared war on him personally, and that all instruments of the government, and particularly the local WarAg committee, were his agents. And Susan veered between the two sets of characteristics that I'd experienced on my first arrival in ways that made life very unpredictable. Some days she would appear kind and considerate towards me, while on other days she acted as if I were collaborating with Anna to snatch Charlie away from her. I had to bite my tongue on several occasions when she was unnecessarily sharp with me. I couldn't do much about how she treated Anna. If I interfered, I was afraid that I would again be reported to Lady Wakeham, and that would be my lot in the Land Army. As for Anna and Charlie, they looked out for every opportunity to be together when his parents were not in sight, which often left me working alone, and sometimes covering for Anna's absence if Roger or Susan turned up to check on us. I did my best, but it did make me feel more tense and alone than I would really care for. Katherine was always given separate tasks from Anna, as if Robert knew that the hostility between her and Anna was not conducive to work. When she worked with me she was mostly placid, but often reminded me of her reason to dislike Anna. She did not want to socialise with me at all.

While I worked in the fields it was obvious from the activity of the British fighters in the air around North Weald that the preparations for the coming battle were going on apace. Planes flew in regularly, and more landed than took off. New planes, I supposed, to replace those lost over the beaches of Dunkirk. News reached us that a bomb had fallen on Brentwood, a nearby town, which seemed to bring the threat from the air a little closer. I wondered if Piotr, and Roger, and the other pilots I had met, would survive whatever was coming. Just thinking about what would happen up there in the skies if another hostile pilot shot at them made me shudder. I sent Roger a card giving him my new address, and asked to be remembered to Piotr, and hoped they were all well.

I also met another resident of the farm. The dairy churns that were picked up and dropped off each day were transported by a man called Will, who was in his late thirties, I'd guess, and who walked with a limp. He lived in an old labourer's cottage about two hundred yards further down the road from the main farmhouse. He was friendly but watchful when I met him one morning after we had started a little late on the milking. Well, the truth is that Charlie had turned up and he and Anna had gone to talk around the back of the barn, leaving me to fetch the cattle in, fix the milking machines to their udders, fill the pails and turn the cows back out to the field when the milking was complete. On my own, it took far longer than if both Anna and I were working together. The result was that Will was standing by his flat-backed lorry smoking as I trundled the cart along the drive to the road. "Why are you so late?" he asked.

I was cross with Anna and Charlie, but I took my anger out on Will with some sarcasm. "Because the cows didn't wake up in time," I answered. Will looked at me uncertainly.

"Don't be so stupid," he said. "If you overslept, just say so."

"I didn't," I answered, "things just delayed me."

"You've delayed the whole round by being late."

"Well, let's get the churns loaded now because you're only making yourself later by complaining. I've been on time every day since I started, but today we ran just a little late. It happens sometimes."

He loaded the churns and tied them to the small fence-like posts and rails that ran down the side of the lorry. "I just need to get the churns loaded in good time and to the dairy," he said. "That's all. They'll be cross with me if I'm late, not with you."

"I'm sorry," I said. "We will be back to normal tomorrow."

"That was good of you, not to drop me in it," Anna said, when I told her what had happened

"We have to stand together sometimes, Anna, but it was Charlie interrupting us that made us late. We should try not to let it happen again. If Will were to complain about us, they'll be watching you even more closely."

"I know. It's just that he knows where I will be all the time, so if he isn't doing anything he can always find me. And today he just woke up early and came to see me."

"Tell him not to interrupt the milking," I urged her. "We've obviously got a deadline for that and can't afford to miss it again."

Anna promised to try to talk to her beau, but it seemed to me that where he was concerned she was all weakness. If he turned up, she didn't know how to send him away to stop him distracting her. And they did not really walk out or go out as a couple, I suppose because of his parents' opposition. Theirs was a semi-clandestine relationship, which perhaps inevitably meant them trying to snatch moments when they could be together.

There were varied tasks to complete on the farm in addition to milking the cattle. There was an apple orchard in which the grass between the trees had to be regularly trimmed, and one day Robert joined us to organise spraying insecticide on the trees. The mixture of insecticide and water had to be just right, he said, and the insecticide itself contained arsenic. I tried, not always successfully, to stay upwind of the spray, therefore, but the hand pump that generated the pressure for the spray to reach the topmost branches and fruit was very hard work indeed. Harder, I think, than a day's hoeing with Lewi, though her companionship had been much more pleasant than a day spent with grumpy Robert, forever complaining about there being insufficient pressure because Anna or I was not working the pump hard enough, and watchful Anna, who always seemed on the lookout for Charlie, even though his father was in close attendance.

We spent several days digging out irrigation ditches, in which Katherine had to join us, because the ditches seemed to collapse regularly and if it were to rain heavily the water would flood the field nearby. I tried to argue with Robert that the sides of the ditches should slope in a shallower form, as I had seen them on some of the farms in Poland, so that the risk of collapse was reduced, but he would not allow it. He claimed it would waste too much valuable land, and what did I know of such matters anyway, when I was just a Land Girl. How could I know more than he, when he had thirty-odd years of experience and I had none. It's the kind of opinion that one experienced a lot, an older and male generation refusing to accept any view from a young female that contradicted their way of doing things. Arguing with him was only likely to cause some complaint against me, so I had to stay silent.

It remained the case that Charlie would turn up and Anna would sneak off with him, leaving me and Katherine digging and throwing up the mud and clay that had fallen into the ditch, or forking up clumps of grass, weeds, twigs and leaves that blocked the water channels. It was easy to become resentful at these moments of abandonment, especially as they were not really moments, but more like hours, and Katherine would tell me how Anna had stolen Charlie's affection when he had at first seemed interested in her and she was much more suitable for him. Sometimes Robert would complain that we had not made enough progress in the time we had been given to do the digging, and I would look to Anna to explain why we had not, but she would just look sheepish and say nothing. I was left to make excuses about stones impeding our progress, or a call of nature delaying us – fictions which it was obvious Robert did not believe, and he would look around the fields to see if he could see his son. Katherine would look contemptuously at the three of us, but she said nothing to Robert.

One morning after milking Katherine and I had pushed the milk churns down to the road ready to be loaded on Will's lorry. Anna had once again disappeared from action when Charlie had appeared, looking sleepy and unshaven. On our return I had started to clean up the dairy, but

Katherine had been looking out for Anna. When she returned a fierce argument broke out, in which Katherine accused Anna of stealing Charlie from her, of falling short in her work, and of failing to satisfy Charlie. It's that last point that I remember most vividly. "He wants what you're not prepared to give him," Katherine said venomously. "I would have let him have me, but you won't. Susan and Robert don't want you with him, but they'd be happy if I was. Why don't you just go back to your parents and leave him to me?" Anna simply turned and walked back to the room she shared with me. The shuddering of her shoulders suggested she was crying. Katherine stood staring at her as she left, and I must have stood staring at Katherine. I'd seen some jealous women, and indeed men, before, but never witnessed such a frank and personal confrontation.

I did not see Piotr or Roger and the other pilots for some weeks. I had sent them that card with my new address in it, and I had also sent one to Lewi, and I managed to meet up with her one Sunday when we both had time off. We met in Epping and had a stroll around the town and out into the countryside on the other side to where I was billeted, before settling in a teashop for a gossip and exchange of news. She told me that things had not changed much since I left Raines Hall. Miss Capthorn still thought that it was her role to act as a combination of headmistress and matron of a boarding school, forever telling her charges what they should and shouldn't do. Her new roommate was a quiet soul who did not want to speak or mix much, so Lewi had been befriending some of the other girls. She did admit that she missed me, even though we had only shared a room and some work for a week. I answered that I missed her even more, and I told her of the awkward relationship between Anna and Charlie, and Katherine's jealousy, and the never-ending conflict that it generated. I confessed to feeling isolated and friendless in my situation, but that I was resigned to sticking with it for the immediate future. I asked her if she knew anything of the pilots from North Weald, and she smiled cheekily and asked me why I should be wondering about them. "Could it be anything to do with that handsome Polish pilot?" she asked. I laughed and guessed that she did have some information, but she teased me for a while, claiming that she couldn't tell me because it could be seen as careless talk. It's true that there was a big campaign to stop people talking about the war in public, but I couldn't see any spies sitting near us in the teashop and I insisted that she tell me what she knew.

"They're not at North Weald the whole time now," she whispered, leaning forward conspiratorially. "One of the Girls I was working with told me that there were rumours of German planes attacking ships and ports in the South of England. So I think that they're down there fighting them off. I was working near the airfield again the other day, but there did not seem to be many planes taking off and landing. You'll have to wait a while to see your Piotr again, I think."

"He's not my Piotr," I protested, but Lewi just gave me a scornful look. I ached a little inside, partly because I so missed Lewi since I had been thrown out of Raines Hall. She had quickly become such a good friend, and I did not have very many of those. I missed her cheerful teasing, her jokes, and of course her re-enactments of scenes from the classics. But I also ached more than a little for Piotr, taking up our nation's fight, and knowing that the next time he took off might be the last thing he ever did. But I was not going to let Lewi know that, though I think she might have worked it out already.

"He'll be back," she said, more softly now, and not teasingly. "I think those two, Roger and Piotr, are going to survive whatever the Jerries throw at them. You'll see them again when they're despatched back to North Weald."

"I hope so," I muttered, "they're just so young, too young...." My voice tailed off, and Lewi took my hand and squeezed it.

"What will we do when they are back?" she asked, trying to cheer me up a little. I had an idea and suggested that the four of us would go to my father's apartment in Victoria, and if he and Henri were back, I would ask Henri to prepare a Polish meal. If they were not, I would do it myself. That was bold of me. I was not the world's worst cook, but I was not far off it. If Henri had been there, he would have laughed uproariously at the thought of me cooking a whole meal for four. Lewi had managed to steer me away from my sadder thoughts though, and she got me to tell her what the best Polish meals were. I told her that they usually consisted of as much meat as was available, sauerkraut, beetroots, turnips, cucumbers, mushrooms, sausages, spices and pepper. If I could obtain some meat, I could probably cobble a meal together, but it would be better if Henri were around. He seemed to know where commodities such as meat could be obtained without ration cards.

With that vague plan formed for a future trip after the pilots returned, we talked of other things, especially the work we had been doing. Lewi had done some work on a farm that was growing fruit and salad vegetables, though she said that the farmer was under some pressure to abandon some of the fruit-growing because it needed too much labour. She had also been cutting back overgrown hedgerows on another farm, where the departure of the labourers had left such routine tasks undone. There had also been some general training provided at Raines Hall, and there was talk of making more formal training courses available in the future. I had not heard anything of this, being billeted on a farm rather than at a hostel. I told her about the spraying of the fruit trees that I had been involved in, and how backbreaking the pump-work was. But I also had to report on the difficulties that Anna was causing by absenting herself from the work. Lewi sympathised with me, but – rather like me – she could not think of any easy way to resolve the problem. Any solution would have to come from the five people who were in constant conflict, and I would just have to watch and hope.

We parted with an embrace, and I thanked Lewi for being such a good friend to me despite our brief acquaintance. "I thought when we met that we were kindred spirits," she said. "And I still think it. Though Piotr might be one as well." She laughed and set off to catch a lift to Harlow, while I turned the other way to walk back to the farm. It was a pleasant and quite sunny afternoon, and I dallied a little to enjoy the sunshine and being in the open. It was hard to believe that we were involved in a war, so pleasant and tranquil was the countryside. But when I reached the farm, and particularly the door to the rooms I shared with Anna, there was a domestic war being fully waged right in front of me. Robert and Charlie were shouting at one another, and clearly Charlie's fondness for Anna was the cause, because Robert was shouting that this was not what he had hoped for his son, and that he could do much better if he gave her up. And Charlie was giving as good as he got, telling his father to mind his own business, and that he would walk out with whoever he chose, and not someone his father might choose for him. The two women were each trying to calm down and quieten their respective men, Anna tugging at Charlie's sleeve to try to haul him away, and Susan speaking quietly to her husband in a voice that I could not hear because of the din made by the two men.

Katherine was not to be seen, though I thought she might be listening somewhere nearby and enjoying the conflict. It was obvious what I needed to do, and I grabbed my uniform and boots and went to the dairy, changing my clothes in the stall there, and then heading for the field to summon in the cattle. Clearly none of those who should have been doing this were going to turn their attention to the mundane task of milking. I did it on my own, even though it was my day off. The shouting died down and the four angry people went off in different directions.

CHAPTER 7
JULY 16TH 1940

I could understand the motives and feelings of all the participants in the domestic conflict to which I was an unwilling bystander. Understand but not really sympathise, that is. For Robert and Susan were parents who had hopes and ambitions for their only child, now a man of course. They wanted him to build on what they saw as their success in owning and running a middle-sized farm at a profit, and they wanted him to gain a place in society that they perhaps (I'm speculating here, I know) did not feel that they had been awarded. I often heard them use phrases such as "Don't throw it all away now" and "You can do much better than her, you know." I was surprised that they were prepared to let me hear this so openly, but I suppose that when your workplace is also your home, it's hard to maintain the same privacy over your domestic squabbles as you would obtain in a more conventional domestic setting.

Perhaps they thought that I might agree with them and give Charlie some additional counsel of my own.

In Charlie's case he clearly wanted to get away from what he saw as his parents', but particularly his father's, dominance. I don't know if he wanted to spend his life as a farmer. It is, after all, seven days a week, fifty-two weeks a year task to keep the farm running. There's little chance or time for pleasurable activities, holidays, theatre trips or other socialising. And it seems to require everyone to wake and rise two hours earlier than is good for one, and not to allow time to administer even the most basic of make-up. Not that Charlie would have wanted to do the last of these, but he did seem to want to do what many other young men do – loiter in pubs, smoke cigarettes with his friends, play some sport, walk down the street with a girl on his arm. He did not seem so dedicated to the rise at dawn, work hours before breakfast, more hours before lunch and yet more hours before dinner, regime that his father favoured. I could even understand why he was fretting at the exemption from war service that he had obtained as a key agricultural worker. He probably took a lot of ribbing about not being in uniform. He had fallen for Anna, and he obviously desired her. Well, she was clearly desirable – I'm sure she turned heads wherever she went. And he was not going to give her up just on account of his parents' wishes.

Katherine had seen her hopes dashed when a much more attractive Girl had turned up at the farm. She was clearly both jealous of Anna and resentful that some early approach of Charlie's had not developed because of her.

I could understand the jealousy, but the intensity of her reactions towards Anna was astonishing, and it impacted on how Robert could deploy us. I thought that she really should have accepted the situation, and perhaps also asked for a transfer, like Mandy before her. Instead, she was potentially volatile at any moment that Anna was around.

I should have sympathised most with Anna. I know that now. She was the inadvertent root cause of the conflict, but it was not her fault at all. Let loose from her parents for probably the first time, she had fallen for the first eligible male to cross her newly independent path. Charlie was attractive, I guess, though he was not as much of a looker as she was. And people would have spoken of him as quite a catch, the only son of an affluent farming family. It was not her fault that Charlie fancied her. Lots of men would have done that. And it was not her fault that his parents had taken against her, and my guess was that she had never faced such hostility and active anger in her life before. She was out of her depth in this environment but could not tear herself away from it because of her feelings for Charlie. I should have befriended her more actively than I did. I was partly annoyed that she was not pulling her weight, which had an impact on me several times a day. I was also concerned that if things exploded, and the Land Army officials were called in, I had to be seen not to be involved. I didn't want another painful interview and punishment. And, I must confess, I was probably also more than a little jealous of her good looks. We all like to be admired. At first glance, and at second glance, she had much more to be admired than I did.

I did sympathise with her when she revealed a particular weakness. It happened one morning after we had finished the milking. Katherine had been sent to do some hoeing on her own, again being kept away from Anna. Robert was waiting for us and told us that Will, the lorry driver who lived nearby, was due to deliver sacks of fertiliser, herbicide, and pesticide. We would need to help him haul the sacks up to the upper floor using the pulley, and then stack them until he needed to use them. He meant to do some spreading in the fields. I had never used such a pulley, and was nervous about it, but Anna from her reaction was clearly even more reticent than I was. She asked if Charlie could do the work instead, but that just made Robert angry. He snapped back at her saying that he didn't know where his son had disappeared to, but that he was paying our wages and we needed to get on with what he asked us to do. He started to show us how the system worked. He went up the upper floor of the barn and lowered the rope that ran over the pulley system. Then he started to attach a sling to the hook that was at the end of the rope. At that moment Will, who collected the churns from outside the farm, manoeuvred his vehicle into the yard. He looked out of the window of his cab and shouted that he'd picked the sacks up the previous day, so he had them on the back of the lorry. We needed to unload them so that he could continue his milk round.

The sacks were heavy, and Anna and I both found it hard to lift them off the edge of the lorry's platform. Will just watched us, smoking a cigarette, and apologising that his bad leg prevented him from lifting such heavy weights. It seemed that the sacks had all been loaded onto the lorry by other men. Robert had continued to attach the sling, and only stood up when he had completed the task. He approached Will's cab, and I heard Will say in a low voice, "Land Girls – are they up to this work?" To his credit Robert did not reply but told Will when we had lifted the last of the sacks, and Will turned the lorry round with an elaborate series of to-ing and fro-ing in the confined space of the yard. He drove off with his inscrutable face as he glanced at us.

Robert then told us that he would place the sacks on the sling one at a time, and we would haul them up using the ropes, but he also needed me and Anna to pull the sling in, lower it to the floor, and unload the sack and stack it against the wall of the barn. He came upstairs with us to demonstrate. Anna hung back as we went up the wooden stairs, and was slow to cross the floor towards the opening through which we would have to pull the sling in. I assumed, wrongly in this instance, that Anna and Charlie had been intending to meet, and to abandon me to complete any work that we were given, and this was the cause of her slowness. She wanted to be with him, not with me straining on the rope. I was seething about their assignations. But I was wrong. Robert did not seem to observe her reluctance, because he was busy getting ready.

He then gave me some gloves so that the fertiliser didn't contaminate me, and the rope wouldn't burn my hands. He gave a similar pair to Anna, who was still slow and reluctant to take part. Robert showed us that we had to wait until the sling was sufficiently clear of the opening to be hauled in. He had a boathook-like device for pulling the sling, or rather the rope above the sling, so that it could then be lowered to the floor, which is when one of us had to take all the strain of the rope. We could then lift and stack the sack and lower the sling to be refilled. It looked simple when he did it without a sack in the sling, but I was not sure that we would find it easy. He went down the stairs to load the first sack, and I hissed at Anna. "What's the matter with you? We both need to work together to get this done. Why are you holding back?"

Anna looked at me with a pained expression. "Vertigo," she muttered. "I suffer from vertigo. I can't go near that opening, and I can't look at the pulley or the sling. What am I to do?"

That stopped me, and I regretted my feelings of antagonism towards her. I thought for a moment or two. "You just haul the rope with me when we have to, and then hold it. I'll pull the sling in and tell you when to lower it. But you'll have to help me by doing that, or we'll never manage." She nodded and seemed near to tears. Again I felt guilty. Down below Robert called up that the first sack was ready. I looked out and down, and he was standing by the sling looking up expectantly. Despite her reluctance, Anna joined me in hauling on the rope, hand over hand, but standing sideways so that she was looking at the side wall of the barn. I stopped hauling when I judged that the sling was high enough and persuaded Anna to hold it tight and still. I took the pole and hook and was just about able to reach above the sling and pull it inwards. Then I asked Anna, who was still not looking at the opening or at the sling, to lower it slowly until it rested on the floor. I suggested that she haul the sack away while I lowered the sling again, since that involved looking through the opening, but she refused at first to move, saying that she couldn't come any closer to the opening. I therefore picked the sack up and handed it to her, encouraging her at least to do the stacking while I lowered the sling. Down below I heard Robert's call when the sling was on the floor, but I had also felt the rope go a little slack and had thought it must have reached him.

In this way, with a few panicky moments when Anna's vertigo seemed to get worse, and with me once losing my grip on the hook and seeing it fly out through the opening, we managed to complete the work. Robert, fortunately for him and for me, had been looking as the hook fell to the floor. He was not cross, for which I was grateful, but just encouraged me that I had to get a very firm grip on the pole, and plant my feet and legs firmly, or the weight of the sack would again wrench the implement from my hands. Once we had stacked all the sacks, and Robert had inspected them to ensure he was content, we were able to get some breakfast. "By the way," Robert said, "I am sorry that Will isn't more sociable. I think it's the accident to his leg – he fell off the lorry when it was raining heavily – and he's hard to hold a conversation with ever since. He lives a pretty lonesome life." I could understand that such an accident could affect someone.

We went to our room to wash, and I apologised to Anna for thinking the worse of her when she was reluctant about the job. She turned and surprised me by hugging me in response, and promptly bursting into tears. When I had comforted her further, and she had wiped the tears away, she said, "It's partly the vertigo. It frightens me and makes me feel light-headed and sick. Thank you for helping me through. I wouldn't have managed it otherwise. But there's also something on my mind, and I wonder if we could talk about it after breakfast. You've been so kind and thoughtful over my vertigo, and I do need some advice." I felt some pangs of guilt at her words. I had not previously been sympathetic to her, and indeed I had on several occasions spoken quite sharply to her. I regarded it as quite normal to help her when she revealed her vertigo, but I could not think how my advice might otherwise be any use to her at all.

After breakfast it was, then, when we took a few minutes back at our quarters before going to see what Richard next wanted us to do, that Anna revealed her other anxiety.

"It's Charlie," she said. Inwardly I sighed, for I'd suspected we were going back to the problem of her relationship with him. But it was not the usual problem. "He wants me to do it with him, to do it with him now." I must have looked nonplussed because she added, "You know, go all the way with him. I've never done that with anyone before, and I don't know what to do about it. He says he wants to join up, and join the war effort directly, but he says he doesn't want to be sent off somewhere without having done it with me. He says it will make us stay together if we do." She looked at me imploringly, as if I was the fount of wisdom that would guide her through this threatening storm of emotion and passion. I said nothing in reply, fearing that I was one of the least well-equipped people to assist her. I really didn't know what to say.

She continued, "I do bring him off when we're together somewhere quiet." She made a gesture with her hand to show what she meant, though I had grasped her meaning. "I've even done that up on the top floor of the barn where we were this morning, of an evening or night when it's dark and we've crept up there. But I'm really scared of going all the way. What if I get pregnant? What if he goes off me? I'd be left up the spout and hopeless."

"What do you think, Ginny?" she asked. She didn't often use my name, mostly talking to me directly. But I suppose the situation we were in, two young women cast up on this farm without any other helpful female company (for I did not think that Susan would be of any assistance to Anna at all, and nor would Katherine), meant that I was the only person Anna could talk to. I've since realised it is a particularly female dilemma. At what point in a developing relationship should we cast our inhibitions, fears, and uncertainties aside and embrace our lover fully? Men generally don't seem to have the same thoughts and emotions about sex. For them it seems to be a more straightforward physical response – they reach a point where they think it's appropriate to go beyond the spooning and petting that characterise the early weeks of the developing love affair. And it seemed that Charlie had reached that point. And there were lots of servicemen already enlisted who shared his view that full sex with their beloved was a necessary part of cementing their long-term commitment.

I did not really know what to say. I felt foolish to mention my mother's lessons for me in the consequences of fooling around, though certain images and sounds from those labour rooms had come instantly to mind. I stalled a little by asking Anna some questions. How and where would they make love if she did agree? In the hay loft of the barn, it seemed, or out in the fields at night, or even in our quarters if I were not there. I shuddered a little at the thought of prickly hay stems being the background to such a moment, but Anna assured me that Charlie would supply blankets. She admitted that her fear of vertigo made her nervous of the barn, but she asserted that it was a good spot because if they entered by the back door, they could not be seen from the farmhouse. Would Charlie take some precautions to prevent Anna becoming pregnant? She said that he had a supply of condoms, "johnnys" she called them, and that he would use them. He had shown her the box to reassure her. Was he going to become engaged to her? Not yet, she said, because it would cause too much trouble with his parents. It would be like a secret engagement, which only the two of them would know about. If Charlie joined up, he would know that Anna was back at home waiting for him. That would be reassuring. "Reassuring for him, you mean?" I asked. "But not necessarily for you."

"Well, what do you think? What's your advice? I need some help in this." Anna asked me, not in any hostile way. She sounded as if I were the only person she could use as a sounding board.

"I don't know what to say to you, Anna," I answered. "I'm not sure that I'm the best person to advise you. I decided some time ago that I would not have sex with a man for a long time because I saw what happened when women have babies. It's frightening, the pain and the experience of giving birth. But I've not had strong feelings for any man, and no man has pressed me to have sex, so I don't know if my determination would hold if I were being pressed as you are. I suppose what I think is that you have to decide if your feelings, not just Charlie's feelings, but your feelings about it are strong enough to let you make love to him. And you need to be confident that he means what he says. If he joins up and is sent off to war somewhere, you'll have months, maybe years, of worry. And if you do go all the way with him, make sure he is wearing one of those johnnys." She nodded, and gave me half a smile. Not exactly confident, but it looked as if she were making up her own mind, which seemed to me to be some kind of good result, however it turned out.

CHAPTER 8
JULY 26TH 1940

The war was getting closer to us. Every day we heard stories of the approach of the Luftwaffe, and we could see in the skies the evidence of the RAF's resistance. There was fighting still over the Channel and Kent, but the German planes seemed to be gradually encroaching along and across the Thames Estuary itself. There were rumours of bombs being dropped on Essex towns, and in the outer suburbs of London. Many people in London, we read, had taken up the government's offer of Anderson shelters, and having bought them were busy installing them in their back gardens. We carried on our work on the farm, and Anna and Charlie carried on their affair. She confided in me that she had not yet agreed to Charlie's pestering requests to make love, but knew it was just a postponement. She feared losing him if she continued to refuse, but she still feared making love to him because of the possible consequences.

On balance, the first fear outweighed the second. Perhaps it was always thus for women, I thought.

It was in the third week of July that I received a card from the airfield. Roger and Piotr had returned from their posting in Kent and the squadron was being re-fitted and re-supplied for a few days. They proposed picking me up one evening, and then calling for Lewi, and going back to their base where the pilots had set up a club room. We could have a few drinks and catch up on events, and then they would return us to our billets in good time. I was grateful for the change that this would represent, and I also told Anna that I would be out for a few hours. Katherine was also away, having been called home because her mother had broken her arm and her father needed her help for a week or more. It was therefore an ideal opportunity for Charlie and Anna to use the room, though there were risks involved, since the door could be seen from the farmhouse. Anna had agreed and had told Charlie.

I pulled out some suitable clothing for the club room – a summer dress and a woollen jacket – and spent a little time making my face up. Anna asked if she could borrow some make up, and we sat together in our bedroom. She was nervous but also happy, I think, and I concluded that tonight was indeed going to provide her and Charlie with the opportunity they, or perhaps it was just he, sought. I offered her some perfume, and she sprayed her neck readily. I suggested that she spray a little in the bedroom, and she smiled gratefully at me and sprayed the air and her bed. I checked the time and realised that Roger would be outside the farm soon. I bent over Anna a little awkwardly, but I hugged her warmly and she did me too. "Good luck," I whispered in her ear. "I hope it …." I didn't quite know how to finish, but she half-laughed at me and whispered her thanks back. Perhaps it's at moments like this that we women understand each other best. I could certainly understand some of Anna's mixed feelings and nervousness. We looked at each other and I think we understood one another better than at any time since I'd arrived at the farm.

Roger and Piotr were sitting in the car outside the farm, so I jumped in the back and chatted to them as we drove out to pick Lewi up. The weather was pleasant, and I enjoyed feeling the wind in my hair. Raines Hall was as school-like as I remembered it, but when the Girls who were enjoying the late sunshine in the garden saw me, some of them came over to me and we exchanged news. Miss Capthorn was as domineering and unsympathetic as ever, and the food was ghastly, but the Girls looked tanned and fit from their labours. I guessed I looked much the same. I missed Lewi coming out, and when I turned back to the car, I saw that she had manoeuvred herself into the front seat next to Roger, and pushed Piotr into the back where he and I would be thrown together on the small back seat. She was incorrigible. Piotr was obviously only too happy to oblige her, and he put his arm around me. That was comfortable. Then he kissed me. That was acceptable. But then I thought of Anna, and wondered how things were going for her. I tried not to get too comfortable alongside

Piotr and wriggled away a little. My personal vow of chastity was still going to hold good.

Piotr talked pleasantly to me for a while, asking me about my work and the farm. I restricted my answers to the work side of things. If I got the chance I might speak more confidentially to Lewi, though I would keep Anna's secret. Roger explained to us that the club room was normally open only for the pilots, a place where they could let off steam I suppose, after being in combat. But because for two or three days the airfield was not operative while the aircraft were repaired and prepared again for fighting, it had been agreed that the pilots could bring their female friends to the club room only. The rest of the airfield was strictly off limits, and we would be in trouble, as would Roger and Piotr, if we were found breaking that rule.

In the club room itself some tables and chairs had been placed on the floor for the comfort of the pilots, and tonight their visitors. A radio played music and gave regular news broadcasts in the background. Lewi and I were not the only young women there. One or two were in uniform themselves, and perhaps had duties at the airfield. Others, like us, were in civvies, and as dressed up as they could be in the circumstances of the war. There was a lot of conversation around us. Friends were obviously taking advantage of meeting socially to catch up with one another.

Roger brought us a round of drinks, and when we sat down, he and Piotr told us all they thought they could about their recent engagements with the Germans. They both felt as if the RAF defences were being tested, as if the Luftwaffe pilots were looking for weak points that could be exploited later. They seemed to engage only briefly, and then to run, and their aircraft were faster than ours, and so following them was not an easy task. There had been exchanges of fire, but both men thought that something much bigger and more dangerous was imminent. They told us a little of what it was like to be under fire, especially by a German pilot who had achieved a better position than theirs, but they praised their aircraft for their manoeuvrability and versatility, and they thought they had better fuel capacity as well. They warned us to be quiet about some of that just in case it was information they shouldn't be sharing with us. They had had some casualties, but only lost two pilots to death. I realised that was another reason why the pilots would have a club room to themselves while there was hostile action. They would need to console each other for the loss of their friends and comrades, and yet be immediately ready to fight again. My heart went out to them as I thought about it.

Lewi regaled us with a series of tales about Raines Hall, Miss Capthorn, and the various farms and farmers and others she had experienced in the weeks since we had last met together. Some of it was very funny. She and another girl had decided on a hot day to have a dip in a nearby pond during their lunch break, thinking that the farm was enclosed, and no-one would see them. But the local vicar had been cycling by, after visiting the farmhouse, and he had assumed that they were in swimming costumes and had stopped to talk to them. At one stage Lewi had thought he was going to stay all afternoon, and that they would have to stay in the pool until evensong, but eventually he exhausted his conversation, and left them. They, of course, had been in their underwear, and hadn't dared to move for the half hour of the vicar's visit. They feared Miss Capthorn's ire if the vicar were to mention them to anyone from the Land Army, but they had got away with it. She and a colleague had been soaked in a fierce rainstorm on one farm, and the farmer – a rather old gentleman it seems – forgot that they were working out in the fields without shelter. Eventually, thoroughly soaked, they had walked back to Raines Hall rather than wait for the lorry to pick them up. Miss Capthorn had something to say about that, of course, but she had to give way when the farmer confessed his memory lapse. A few of the Girls had found the work too hard – blisters, aching muscles, minor injuries were all common among them – and had been allowed to return to their previous lives. But most of the Girls were coping, and anticipating the harvest season that was to come. "Let's hope it's a good harvest," said Roger, "and not interrupted by the Luftwaffe."

Lewi and I shared the cost of a second round of drinks, but then somehow she and Roger moved away from us temporarily and left Piotr and me on our own. I said she was incorrigible! Piotr became more serious, changing to speaking in Polish, and telling me that he was often frightened in the cockpit of his fighter. The fear would come before any dogfight, not during one, because there was no time to think of anything else while the fight was on. I said that I imagined that many of the pilots would experience similar feelings. He agreed and said that they each had their own way of dealing with it. When he had been flying in Poland, against the Germans, he had countered it by imagining himself back home after the war was over and the Germans had been driven away. False hopes! Now, he said, he got rid of the fear by thinking of the next time he would see me. I winced. I almost cried out. This was not what I wanted to hear. I liked Piotr, and I sympathised with him deeply for what he was doing in fighting with our forces, but I feared for his life, and I was particularly afraid that any commitment made between us would lead to terrifying grief and anguish. I had suffered enough through my separation from my mother, and was still suffering from it, I suppose, and I did not want to amplify the loss and sorrow that was caused by missing her so much. If Piotr had to die, as so many of the pilots were condemned to do, I wanted it to be before we had fallen in love with one another. I wanted to protect myself as much as possible. It was a selfishness that I am now ashamed to recall, but it was how I felt.

I did not try to tell Piotr all that I felt. It seemed to me that I would just provoke more earnest pleading from him. I said in as light a way as I could that I was always happy to see him and to share his company. I liked being with a Polish man and speaking the language again. I wanted to work for the war effort, and I wanted the war to be over. I like him hoped to go back to Poland, because I could look for my mother then. "But," I said, "I don't want a firm relationship until the war is over. I need to be free to do whatever comes up. I will keep seeing you as long as that is possible. If you have to go away, or if I do, I want us to be able to do so without being upset."

He claimed that he understood my feelings, and that he would respect them. He said that he especially wanted to continue to see me when possible. But he thought that even when the war finished, it would not be possible to go back to Poland. He did not expect to see his home again. The Russians would take over, and they hated men like him. And women like me. He hoped my mother would escape somehow. He also said that he thought the coming battles in the air would be the most important moment of the war, more significant even than saving the Expeditionary Force from Northern France. "If we lose in the air, Ginny," he said, "think what will then happen on the ground. And there's another thing. It's been good that you could come to the Club Room tonight, but the airfield is a dangerous place." He leaned in more closely to me and spoke more quietly. "It's obvious to me that the Germans will next attack the airfields. Our defences here are not strong enough. The buildings are weak and the shelters are poor. I have told the commanders here that that's what I fear. They say they've done everything possible, but that does not seem right to me. If they attack, I would rather be in the air than on the airfield. I probably shouldn't be saying this, so don't tell others what I've said. I hope to meet you somewhere else, not here."

I was prevented from replying by Lewi and Roger returning. "Well, well, you look cosy," she teased. It was true that as Piotr had said these last words our heads had almost touched. I no doubt looked embarrassed and probably my face flushed red. Piotr just smiled, as he always did when Lewi teased us, and drew back.

I decided it was time to put my plan to entertain us all to a meal into action. I checked with Roger, who confirmed that the refitting and repairing would finish on Sunday, and the squadrons would be back in action on Monday. "Right," I said, "I'd like to invite you to a meal at my father's flat on Sunday. I will go there early and start cooking. And Roger can drive you there and drive us all back as well. I don't know if my father will be there. He can't tell me where he is most of the time now. If he's there I'm sure he'll be interested to talk to you."

Shortly after that we all agreed it was time for us Girls to be returned to our lodgings. We did not want to get Lewi into any trouble with Miss Capthorn, so we drove to Raines Hall first. Once again Lewi manoeuvred me into the back with Piotr, and we were squashed together on the rear seat. Piotr stretched his arm around the back of the seat, but once we were moving his arm came down to my shoulder, and he squeezed me even more closely to him. I tried to make pleasant conversation, while he just looked at me with what was now becoming a familiar smile. When I stopped speaking, he kissed me, quickly at first and then more deeply. "Don't waste any time, you two," Lewi laughed at us. She never missed a trick, did she?

Piotr whispered in my ear as we drove back towards Epping. He was becoming bolder, and he first kissed me on the ear and then he placed his tongue in my ear. I did not find it unpleasant, in fact it gave me a momentary thrill, especially the physical familiarity and suggestion of intimacy, but I did note for myself that he was making progress in whatever campaign he was mounting. I needed to be careful. As we reached the farm, he was again kissing me, and his tongue was now stroking mine, and again I felt the excitement of his passion. My hand fell on his lap, and I realised that he had a prominent erection. I let my hand rest there, and even stroked his penis gently through his trousers. I'm not sure I was being as careful as I ought. When the car stopped, I jumped out and waved my goodbyes.

Anna was in bed as I entered our bedroom, but she had stayed awake. She wanted to share her news. She had been crying. She told me that it had all seemed to go well at first with Charlie, but when the moment came she had been hurt as he tried to enter her. She had reacted badly and stopped him. He was upset then angry. He had fled after shouting at her and had managed to escape from the room. She had not seen him since. She had stayed in the bed, crying and worried that all had gone wrong. I tried to comfort her, saying that this must have happened to thousands, indeed millions, of women. There was nothing new in the world, and her pain was something that we could all understand. Charlie would have to be more careful if they tried again. This seemed to comfort her a little, and she lay back and shut her eyes as if trying to sleep. As I got into my bed I thought of Piotr. Would we find ourselves in the same position as Anna and Charlie? I was surprised by myself since I had not until then imagined myself in bed with Piotr. I was also surprised to have received such intimate secrets from Anna, who in my first weeks at the farm had exuded mostly silence and little friendliness, but for whom I now felt a deep sympathy and some responsibility to support. In the face of the probing and advancing Luftwaffe, things were clearly changing and developing rapidly in our world, but where it would all end I did not know.

CHAPTER 9

JULY 27TH-28TH 1940

As we sat at breakfast next morning, having completed the milking and left the full churns at the farm entrance, I told Susan of my plans for the meal at my father's. Susan was in her more positive mood towards me and said that I should purchase the food in Epping that morning, for fear that it would run out before I could buy it, and that she would ask Robert to let me go into London that afternoon. Transport around the capital city was getting worse, with shortages of staff and of fuel affecting services. Sunday, being generally a non-working day, was suffering the most. I could see the logic of this proposal and was grateful for her assistance.

Susan directed me to the shops where she had registered my ration card and gave the card to me to use in purchasing the food. She said I should be able to buy most of what I said I needed – milk, butter, bread, cheese, eggs, sugar – but when I said I wanted to buy beef she shook her head. She did not think there would be any joints of beef left on a Saturday. People had taken to buying their meat for roasting on a Friday, to make sure of obtaining it. She told me to ask, nevertheless, because the butchers were sometimes holding meat back in the cold room behind the shop, but she would phone around the local farms. I knew that between them the farms exchanged and sold produce that never entered the general supply to shops. I was grateful for her help, but as it happened, I didn't need it. I looked pleadingly at the butcher, and suggested how important the meal was to be, and he said, "Okay, for a Land Girl, I'll find you a roasting joint. I don't often serve Land Girls. I suppose you're all too busy toiling in the fields."

I said my farewells at the farm thanking Susan for her help and returning my ration card. Anna had offered to do all the milking to cover for me. Even if she had to join Katherine in doing it. "I'll persuade Charlie to help me if he's still talking to me, and Katherine will avoid us if he does," she said. I gave her a hug, which she appreciated, and set off to the station.

Susan was right about the transport. Even on a Saturday it was disrupted and slow. The wait at Epping and at Leytonstone was much longer than usual, and the trains themselves moved only slowly towards their destinations. In the end it took me two and a half hours to reach my father's flat, and the weight of the two bags of food had tired me out. The flat was quiet. Neither my father nor Henri was there. They were obviously away somewhere on the business of ensuring the country had enough planes to defend itself. I made some tea, ate some bread and cheese, and had a long soak in the bath. Then I went to bed early and fell deeply asleep.

I didn't hear my Father and Henri return. It must have been quite late. I was very pleasantly surprised, therefore, when Henri brought me an early morning tea on the Sunday. "You are going to cook a meal, Miss Virginia?" he asked politely. Henri was always polite. I could never detect any irony in his words or tone, though at times there must surely have been some. This was probably one such instance.

"Yes, Henri. I've invited three friends for lunch, but I think there will be enough for you and daddy. He is here, isn't he?" Henri nodded. "My friends are coming at half-one, so what time should I start cooking?"

"Were you going to slow roast the beef?"

"Yes, and to make a vegetable stew, a Polish one if I can. One of my friends is a Polish pilot. He's flying with the RAF. I thought he would enjoy that."

"The beef will take about two and a half hours and needs to stand for a while after cooking. The stew will be less, but you need to add different vegetables at different times. Have you brought some herbs? I couldn't see any."

Herbs! Of course I hadn't brought any. I hadn't really been thinking sufficiently. Once I'd solved the problem of buying the basic provisions, and the joint of course, I hadn't given the cooking any further thought at all.

Henri could see my disappointment and self-reproach. He was always able to tell my feelings, even if I said nothing.

"I'll find those for you. And I'll serve some breakfast in," he paused to consult his watch, "thirty minutes. Your father will be up then. He wants to visit the Air Ministry this morning."

"Is it open on a Sunday?" I realised how stupid the question was before I'd finished it. "I know, I know, there's a war on, and there will be fighting in the air even though it's Sunday. Will he be back for lunch?"

"Yes I think so, because I told him last night that I thought you were planning a meal. He said he would be most interested to eat it." Although I could never detect Henri's irony, I could hear my father's even as Henri repeated his words.

"Right then, I'd best make it an interesting meal, hadn't I? But you mustn't tell him, or my friends, if you give me some help." Henri smiled and went to prepare breakfast. I dressed quickly and went to read the Sunday paper before my father insisted on his rights over it during breakfast. The news was not encouraging though. Our fighters were attempting to resist the Germans, but the Luftwaffe was increasingly bold in its attacks and incursions. The journalists reported the bare facts and did not offer interpretations.

Over breakfast, after greeting him with a double kiss and a hug and bringing him up to date on my work on the farm, I tried to get my father to tell me what he thought of the present situation. He put aside his paper and asked if there was any particular reason for my enquiry. I told him that I had met up with Roger, and with a Polish pilot, who were based for some of the time at North Weald airfield, near the farm. They had been fighting over Kent and the English Channel. So I wondered what was coming next.

"Something much bigger, I fear," my father said. "And much more deadly. Is there anything to these friendships, Ginny? Or anything more than just friendship?"

How do parents know our secrets even though we haven't mentioned them? Haven't given even the slightest inkling of them? I tried to sound dismissive. "No, not really. I wouldn't want a relationship with someone serving in the armed forces at this time. Too much risk of suffering I suppose."

My father looked more closely at me for a few seconds. "Especially an RAF pilot, Ginny. They must be the riskiest of all. But I fear we will all be at risk soon, though I can't say any more about that. Are these two pilots coming here for lunch?" When I nodded, he said that he'd look forward to speaking to them. He made as if to return to reading the paper, but I interrupted him with my usual incomplete question.

"I don't suppose there's any news of...?" Incomplete because we both knew whom I was referring to. He shook his head, sighed a little, and picked up the paper. I finished my breakfast and picking the plate and cup up, went to join Henri and to be inducted into the art of Polish cookery.

Henri had found a large roasting dish, one with a cover, and he showed me how to prepare some root vegetables as a base for the beef, and then to brown the beef prior to putting it in the oven. As we worked I asked him what he thought was the reason my mother had not ever taught me how to cook. His answer – she was raising me to be a lady, not a cook – was said in the most matter-of-fact manner, as if there were no doubt that was the reason. Well why then, if she was raising me to be a lady, had she made me work for a whole summer, three months, on the farms? Henri looked at me for a few seconds. He knew my argument was weak. Then he gave the same reply – that she was raising me to be a lady. I gave the argument up. Henri trumped me by asking what I was using for stock. Stock! Same as the herbs, I'd completely forgotten I would need stock. Fortunately for me, Henri had a jug of stock at the back of the large American refrigerator that dominated one half of the kitchen. I was obviously doing quite well in my preparations to be a lady. I couldn't organise the first thing as far as cooking went. Well maybe the first thing, the main ingredients. But beyond that, I was a complete lady-like failure.

Henri said that he had found a couple of bottles of my father's champagne, and he had put them in the refrigerator. He said that we could go down to the cave to get some red wine. He insisted on calling the large walk-in cupboard in the building's cellar a cave, as in the French. And he had a surprise for me in the cave. So once we had started to cook the beef, and to gently sauté the first vegetables, we traipsed down the stairs and into the depths of the building's red brickwork. My father kept some wine on a large rack that stood against the back wall of this cave. He kept various outdoor items such as his golf clubs, wellington boots, walking boots and shoes, a shooting stick, well you get the picture. But when Henri opened the door to the cave there was a splendid black and silver, second-hand ladies cycle. It had a basket at the front, and a comfortable looking saddle. "I persuaded your father that you would find this useful. We found it on one of our forays. I imagined that you might find it useful. Getting around can't be easy, and we know that in London it's getting more difficult as well."

I was delighted. It would give me a mobility around Epping and its environs that I had not had. I thanked Henri and hugged him, telling him that he had been as thoughtful and helpful as ever. While he fished around for some wine at the back of the cave, I slung my leg over the saddle and tried the cycle out for size. It seemed perfect for me. He said to leave the cycle in the cave until I could take it with me, but I said that I would persuade Roger to attach it to his car and take it back for me that evening. We returned to our cooking, and Henri opened one of the bottles of red wine we had carried upstairs and added it to the stock, along with some herbs. I felt no guilt about him doing this rather than I. I was practising being a lady!

The dinner was actually a great success, though I say so myself. The champagne was cold and its freshness cut through our palates with an exciting tingle. The quick intoxication encouraged everyone to talk animatedly. My father chatted first to Lewi about being a Land Girl, and she was spirited about the work, though rather scathing of the authorities. I shook my head to indicate that I had not told my father about my mishaps, but she repeated her story about being caught by the vicar, or rather not caught by the vicar, swimming in her underwear. That distracted him from any thought of me.

Then my father talked to the two men, asking them about their aircraft, the airfield they were based at and others they had used. Since they knew that my father was working on the supply of aircraft, they were happy to answer his questions. Yes the German planes were faster, but much less agile in combat. It meant that our pilots had a good chance in a dogfight, though you never knew when another enemy plane would surprise you. But when the Germans turned tail and headed for home, which was quite soon because of their poor fuel supply, it was not possible easily to give chase. Roger said that Piotr always wanted to approach the German planes more closely than the RAF tactical advice allowed them. Piotr said that was the lesson he had learned from the defeat in Poland. It served no purpose to hang fire and keep a distance between the planes. My father was particularly interested by that. Piotr mentioned his concern about the defences of North Weald. My father said that he did not know much about that aspect of the RAF, but he was obviously not surprised by the intransigence of the commanding officers. He'd encountered intransigence at every level, he complained, just at the point in our history when some more flexibility would help us. He would mention it to someone he knew at the Ministry. He doubted, though, that it would result in any change. He was in awe, he said, of all those who were flying in combat. The country was depending on that small group of men, their courage, their bravery and their skill, and he said that he felt privileged to sit down to eat with two of them. I had to dry my eyes as I went in search of the food.

Henri had managed the food perfectly, and allowed me to take much of the credit, quite undeservedly. Piotr claimed it was a great reminder of good Polish food, which was just what I wanted to hear. My father lived up to his admiration of the pilots by plying them with his best burgundy, to the point where I had to remind him that Roger had to drive us back. After our meal we took a walk across to St James' Park passing Bucking ham Palace, and then went down to Westminster. Standing by the bridge there, on a delightful summer day, the only reminder of the war was the barrage balloons, floating high over us, and the number of people in uniform. It seemed hard to believe that Roger and Piotr would next day once again be risking their lives up in that blue-and-white sky.

Piotr asked me to sit with him for a while in a small garden behind the Houses of Parliament. Roger took Lewi off to show her Westminster Abbey quickly. Or perhaps Lewi persuaded Roger to take her away for a few minutes. That was more likely. Once again Piotr tried to tell me of his strong feelings about me. And once again I had to tread a narrow path between discouraging him, on account of my own fears, and encouraging him by allowing him so show me how passionately he felt. His kiss seemed in danger of overwhelming me. His hand cupped my breast and I did not want to stop him. But I did not toy with him. I still felt guilty about our previous encounter. I did not dare let him think that I would, as Anna had put it to me when talking of her Charlie, go all the way with him. I felt too vulnerable, and I knew how vulnerable he was. I was resisting falling in love, however much he had fallen.

We went home for some tea, and then Roger drove us back across London. He lashed my cycle to the boot of his car with some rope, and he took a circuitous route across town, through the West End and Regents Park, past Camden and Finsbury Park and across the marshes and reservoirs at Walthamstow. In all those places people were enjoying the last of the sunshine of the day, and except for the prevalence of uniform, and the gun batteries we passed, you would not have known that we were at war. How quickly that illusion was dispelled.

CHAPTER 10
JULY 29TH-AUGUST 20TH 1940

Next morning Robert took delivery of a large old wooden table. He told us that we were to put it in our living room, and he would help us to build some sides to connect to the legs so that the whole construction provided shelter from blasts and shrapnel. If the sirens went off at night, or if any bombing started, we would need to crawl beneath it and sleep there. He was also going to reinforce the cellar of the farmhouse, which he had already started to prepare as a shelter for himself, Susan, Charlie and Katherine. I guessed that part of the motivation to provide shelter for us Girls was to keep Anna and Charlie separate if nocturnal air raids required us to take shelter, and if it was true that he favoured Katherine, putting Charlie near her might help that particular cause. But I also thought that in the light of Piotr's fears, it was probably sensible to take some steps, however small, to improve our defence on the farm. North Weald was not that far away, and in one conversation Piotr had told me that bomber pilots often dropped their bombs away from their intended targets. The targets were often defended by guns on the ground, which meant high risk to the bombers; nearby villages and towns were not so defended, and were much less of a risk therefore.

The converted table was, in Robert's view, much better than an Anderson shelter, which had been given free to many low-income families and which others had purchased from the government. He had considered buying one of those, but the corrugated iron sheets looked very flimsy to him, and he thought that we might be less likely to use one on a cold or wet night since it would involve traipsing across to wherever we had planted it in open ground. An Anderson shelter would often be wet inside, he had heard, and uncomfortable for its occupants. The table was solid enough to resist some fall of plasterwork and debris, though if there was a direct hit, well.... I was almost stupid enough to ask what if there was a direct hit, but I realised what he meant. If a bomb was a direct hit on the building you were in, whether the farmhouse cellar, our living room, or an Anderson shelter in a garden, then the occupants were very likely to die. We were protecting ourselves from a nearby bomb strike. And Robert was ensuring that Anna and Charlie would never share an Anderson shelter. I guessed from this that he and Susan had not realised the intimacy the couple had attempted. I suspected that Anna would have been banished from the farm if they'd discovered that.

Robert showed us what he wanted to achieve on all four sides of the table. He helped us to construct a frame from wood that he brought in from the barn, and to attach chicken wire in double spread across the frame. Then we had to drill holes in the frame and just into the underside of the table, before screwing the frame into position. I could see that the whole construction would look like a cage. Having showed us how to build one long side of this cage, he left us to make the other long side and two ends on our own, telling us to call him when the final end-piece was ready to be fitted. This took rather longer than the first side, and we worked well into the afternoon to complete the task. Making the frames was not too hard, though neither of us had any previous experience of woodwork. But drilling the holes in the frame to match the small holes in the underside of the table was very difficult. Neither of us could easily manage the drill lying on our backs as Robert had done, and we went wrong time and time again in trying to fit the frames to the right point on the table. Eventually we were able to call him across, and he produced two hinges which he fitted to the second end-piece of the frame. He showed us that we would be able to crawl into the area under the bed, and pull the end-piece into position, so protecting ourselves on all four sides. Then we could sleep. He would ask Susan to find us a mattress to put under the table so that it was softer for us. All in all, it seemed not a bad attempt to protect us.

Within a few days Anna and I had recourse to use the table. The Battle of Britain, or the Battle for Britain? I don't particularly care which you call it. But we were close enough to be deeply affected by the events of the following weeks. Luftwaffe bombers were attacking coastal airfields and radar stations, but also started to probe the defences of London and the surrounding suburbs and countryside, and fighters from both sides screamed and roared in the skies as the RAF tried everything to resist the enemy. Night bombing started, and some German planes found their way into the centre of the city and dropped bombs there. We retaliated, and the stakes seemed to be increasing every day. The first time the sirens sounded in Epping was at night. Anna woke me to warn me of their sounding. We stumbled in the dark across our room and through to the cage, as we'd come to call it. We got in and lay on the mattress, but despite it being summer, it was chilly without our bedclothes. I went back and retrieved some blankets from both our beds. I hadn't shared a mattress with anyone for some years. It felt unusual, and Anna turned her back on me perhaps because of that unfamiliarity. But in the morning when I heard our alarm clock sounding in the bedroom, Anna was lying close to me and one arm was around me.

I feared for Roger and Piotr, because I followed the news broadcasts and even tried to obtain a newspaper to keep abreast of events, and I knew how heavy the fighting had become. North Weald airfield seemed constantly to be busy, with flights of fighters regularly taking off and landing. We heard and saw them in the sky, either heading south to search for the Luftwaffe, or returning to the airfield to refuel and, if possible, to rest. There were daily counts of the number of our planes lost and the number of enemy aircraft destroyed. Pilots were dying in large numbers, or they were severely injured or burned as their planes crashed. But I heard nothing from North Weald until a card arrived telling me that Roger had been injured and was spending some time on administrative duties. Piotr, however, was still well. Somehow he was surviving the carnage all around him. I remember Roger saying when we first met that Piotr was a good pilot. Perhaps that was saving him. And what kind of euphemism was "Injured"? Had Roger been shot down, and perhaps had to parachute to the ground? Or had he been wounded by a stray bullet? I could not find out more because Roger told me that I could not meet them until things calmed down. All leave had been cancelled, and there was no down time. I replied wishing him well and offering my love to them both. Funny isn't it, how casually we may offer love, when perhaps we just mean good will? If Roger told Piotr that I had sent my love to him, how might he think of that?

To ease my anxiety I took to cycling in the evening, at first just in the vicinity of the farm, and then taking in the villages around Epping. Although I was generally much more fit after five or six weeks as a Land Girl, I found that some muscles in my legs had not been developed by the work. Cycling was painful after a half hour or so, and my legs would remain sore for a day or two, but I thought that would pass. If I cycled to a vantage point on high ground I could see the fighters taking off and landing at North Weald at closer range, but there were no hills overlooking the airfield directly. The airfield itself was under constant guard. My uncertainty about my relationship with Piotr seemed to affect me particularly during those weeks. When Hornchurch Airfield was bombed, just a few miles to the south of us, I realised how close to home the Luftwaffe was reaching. I hoped that the commanders at North Weald had heeded Piotr's warnings about the ground defences and the buildings.

One afternoon I asked Anna to cover the milking because I wanted to ride out to Raines Hall. I felt that talking with Lewi might ease the anxiety that I was experiencing. Anna didn't mind, and said that she would again persuade Charlie to assist her. It was odd – in my first weeks I'd found Anna shirking and avoiding the work at times. Now, if it meant that if I would be absent for a few hours, she would take on the extra work. How a couple of confidential conversations had changed things. She had told me that things were uneasy between her and Charlie. They were still meeting one another, and it remained uncertain in her mind whether or not she would attempt another full liaison with him soon.

It was hard work cycling to Raines Hall. The wind was gusting, and as I tired I found it more difficult to control the bicycle. I almost slipped into a ditch as I neared my goal, but I managed to stay upright and to turn away from the ditch edge. I arrived at Raines Hall just a few minutes before the lorries returning the Girls to the Hall, and so I waited by the lawn, sitting on a bench there. Miss Capthorn came out of the house and made towards me as if she would greet me – I was still in my uniform – but when she recognised me, she turned swiftly around and headed back indoors. It was probably as well that she did. I'm not sure that I would have been very polite. I missed Lewi, and I had found Houblions Hill Farm a difficult place to work in. And all because of her.

Lewi, and one or two of the other Girls, on the other hand were delighted to see me. They were suntanned from working so much in the fields, and we spent some time comparing notes on the various farm work we had been asked to undertake. The Girls all seemed to know about Piotr, and I teasingly complained to Lewi about what she had told them. One said that she envied me – the average age of the men she had been meeting was sixty or more. Could I introduce her to a good-looking pilot instead of Lewi? I promised to bear that in mind.

When they went in to prepare for dinner, I managed to find a few minutes to talk to Lewi. I told her how anxious I was about the two pilots. She said that she too had received a card from Roger. He hadn't told her any more than he had me, and she too had wondered how exactly he had been injured. The Girls working near North Weald had told her of aircraft returning to the base with smoke trailing behind them. One had even been clearly on fire. But there had been no sound of a crash. They knew that some aircraft had been lost and some pilots injured or killed in action in Kent and above the Channel. She also told me that she had said to Roger that she could not think that any long-term relationship between them was possible. Their backgrounds, she thought, were just too different. He had accepted this and had even said he was grateful for what she'd said. However, he was content if she would still accompany him, especially if all four of us were meeting. He liked her company, found her to be interesting to talk to, and he liked dancing with her or feeling her on his arm as they walked together. He said that in the circumstances of the war, it was a pleasure for him to know her. His words, it seemed to me, had been gracious and sensitive. Part of me wished that Piotr had been able to accept the same, while another part of me thought that Lewi's arrangement with Roger would never have satisfied him. Or me, I realised. I talked to Lewi a little about my dilemma, although I knew she might tease me about it at some later date. She said that I would just have to leave it to time to determine what happened, but she agreed that fighter pilots were the most likely people in the world to disappear suddenly and completely from our lives. There was every reason to take things slowly.

I did not go into dinner with Lewi. I did not want to see Miss Capthorn. I had brought a sandwich which Susan had made for me, and I said that I would stop and eat it on my way home. We hugged, said how much we missed each other, and I set off for Epping. The wind was at my back now, and I was more easily able to control the bicycle in the gusts that filled out my blouse. I reached the farm just as it was getting dark and walked around the nearby fields for a while to sort out my thoughts. I could see that I was perhaps on the brink of falling in love with Piotr, which surprised me. But his strength of character, having survived all that the War had thrown at him, and his gentility towards me, but also his passionate interest in me, were all working towards that end.

CHAPTER 11

AUGUST 24TH-25TH 1940

It was hard to concentrate on our work at times. The great battle that was being fought to save the country now seemed to be on our very doorstep. The fighters from North Weald often circled the fields where we worked as they headed for the fighting in Kent or elsewhere. And each time I saw them I wondered which one was Piotr's Hurricane, and whether he would return safely in two- or three-hours' time.

Saturday August 24th was the worst of such days. It had been a warm and sunny day, and Anna and I had been working on one of the ditches at the furthest extremity of the farm. It had partly collapsed, and the earth had impacted, so that digging it out and trying to reshape it had taken all day since milking. We had just started to walk back to the farm buildings to gather the cows in, walking quickly because we were late and the cattle would be moving of their own volition towards the holding pen, desperate to unload the burdens of their udders. Anna heard the noise first and stopped me. It was the air raid siren. What should we do, she asked me. I was not sure, but decided on balance we were better off staying in the fields and risking a stray bomb, rather than being caught around the buildings if a bomb struck them. Next we heard the drone of many aircraft, somewhere behind us. And shortly after that there were flights of German fighters and fighter bombers, and then we saw the North Weald Hurricanes flying towards the Germans. They engaged with each other briefly, and the Hurricanes flew off a little to the south, circling so as to return to the fray. All this was high in the sky, but then the German squadrons flew lower, turned over Epping and headed towards the airfield. "Oh God," I cried, "they're going to attack North Weald." Shortly after that they were lost to our sight.

The Hurricanes came back and followed them, and then they too disappeared. Anna could see that I was upset, more so than just by the sight of the enemy aircraft. And then we heard the explosive crash of the bombs, even at the distance that we were from the airfield. The noise seemed to carry in the clear summer air. The contrast was so extreme. There were we in an almost idyllic green pastoral scene, the cows in the distance gathering to be milked. And just a couple of miles away death and destruction had fallen on the small village of North Weald and the brave airmen and soldiers it hosted. It took me a few minutes to overcome the initial shock, but after the all-clear sounded we agreed that all we could do was get on with the milking. The Luftwaffe were not interested in our farm and the people and animals there. They were after a much bigger prize.

Over dinner I wondered whether I should cycle towards the airfield, but Robert persuaded me not to. "They'll have closed the approach roads," he said, "and you'd just be seen as in the way of the ambulances and the wardens."

"But I know two of the pilots there," I protested.

"They might let you past the roadblocks if you could prove you were next of kin, but not otherwise."

I therefore had to lie on my bed and worry about what might have happened. Next morning Robert came out to join us in doing the milking. He said that he had gone into Epping fairly late in the evening to find out more about the bombing and its aftermath. He said that not much was yet clear, but that some buildings on the airfield and in the village had been destroyed. There had been several deaths, and wounded personnel had been ferried to the hospital, but beyond that not much else was precisely known to those gathered on the High Street. The airfield had survived the bombing and was still fully operational. The Germans had obviously failed in their main objective, probably because the Hurricanes had got into the air in time to attack them. "Thank God for the Watch," said Robert. "They would have tracked the Nazis right across Kent and Essex. Then the controllers could warn the airfield and get the siren sounded." He asked us about the siren, and we said that we'd heard it but judged it better to stay where we were. Once the aircraft had headed towards

North Weald, we had felt safe to return, and after the all-clear we had completed the milking.

After breakfast I decided to cycle into Epping and attend mass at the Catholic church. All I could offer to the battle was prayer. After mass I talked to some of the parishioners and listened to what they had to say about the attack. Some of them lived near North Weald, and it was true that both the village and the airfield had lost buildings. The Post Office and the Woolpack pub had been destroyed, and those who knew the airfield said that the Officers' Mess and the living quarters had been bombed. Worse than that, a number of soldiers from the Essex Regiment, whose job it was to man the guns in defence of the airfield, were rumoured to have been killed by a direct hit. And it was believed that two villagers had been killed as well. "Bastards," one of the men said, disregarding the ceremony he had just attended. "Fucking German bastards." None of us standing around felt inclined to criticise his words.

I hung around in Epping for a while, and even toyed with riding on to Raines Hall to see if Lewi had by chance stayed there on her day off. But I concluded that she was likely either to have gone off with some of the other Girls, or to have visited her family, who after all were close by. My indecision was interrupted by the sudden and alarming sound of the air raid siren once again. I should have sought out one of the communal shelters that had been constructed for just such events, but something drove me to pedal as quickly as I could out of Epping and into the surrounding forest areas where there were no buildings and no targets, therefore, for the German bombers, whether they were still striving to reach the airfield or just casually dropping their loads and not risking the gunfire of the airfield.

I found that I had taken one of the roads that lead, a little circuitously, towards the airfield itself. The roads all round that area often pass directly through the ancient Epping Forest, the old hunting forest of English kings and queens. I had cycled along several of them as I explored the area. In high summer the forest is an intriguing place. Where it is forested the leaf canopy is so thick that very little light gets in and it is almost as dark as night. Where there are clearings or wide paths for horses to be ridden through the forest, shafts of light break through the darkness. It reminded me of passages of Wordsworth I had read at school, or of an Italian painter my art teacher had always spoken of and shown us prints of in her art history books. "Chiaroscuro, girls," she would say, "dark and light, like life itself!" As I looked into the threatening gloom from the roadway, my thoughts and fears were as dark as the forest itself. Not much chiaroscuro lurked in me as I cycled.

Once I had clearly left Epping behind, I slowed down and gave myself more time to think. I was evidently drawn towards the airfield because of Piotr, and I suppose Roger, and some inner desire to help them, or protect them, or comfort them. But that hope was really in vain. If the Germans were about to attack the airfield again, there was nothing I could do to stop them. I would not even be allowed into the airfield and would need to get into a public shelter if the bombers came over again. Just as my thoughts were clearing, I came to a roadblock. Two wardens had parked a lorry across the road, and they indicated that I should stop. One of them approached me. "Sorry miss, you can't go any further at the moment unless you're a North Weald resident. The bombing yesterday has left a lot of damage. And to add to that, we think that there may be another attack. We're not sure if we heard the sirens sound a little while ago."

Just at that moment we both stopped to listen. We could hear the drone of a number of approaching aircraft. "There you are," he said sadly," sounds like they've come back again. You should really be in a shelter."

"Yes, I think I got a little lost. All these forest roads look alike."

"Best just sit in the lorry while any attack is on. Nowhere's fully safe but at least there'd be some protection against a blast."

I left my cycle on the ground and climbed up into the back of the lorry. There were two bench seats attached to the sides, and I sat on one and the two wardens sat on the other. They were a friendly pair. Too old to join up, they had given their time to the ARP, they told me. They lived in Woodford but had been called out to North Weald because of the emergency after the air raid. They congratulated me on being a Land Girl and serving the country. From their knapsacks they produced sandwiches and a thermos flask of tea, and they shared their victuals with me. Meanwhile the noise of the approaching aircraft had become louder, and the bombers seemed to be passing almost directly overhead.

"It is North Weald, then," one of them said. "They're after all the airfields." I therefore had to sit in the lorry and chat to them as the airfield suffered its second day of attacks. We could hear the defensive guns firing, and at times the noise in the air grew louder, and then the noise abated as the aircraft drew away. The two wardens speculated that a fierce dogfight was probably going on. "Our pilots will be trying to get at the bombers, and the Jerry fighters will be trying to stop them. Close combat for aircraft. Very dangerous." His words did not comfort me, and my anxiety increased as time went on. Our conversation died out. We were probably all wondering about the dead and wounded from the aerial battle.

After an hour or so things in the air seemed to go quiet. We climbed down from the lorry. The road and the forest were silent. In the distance we could hear the all-clear siren sounding. "Time for you to go home, miss," the warden said. "But not this way. No-one can go towards the airfield."

So I had to mount the cycle and pedal back the way I had come, into Epping and out to the farm. And as I did so, tears trickled slowly down my cheeks, and I did nothing to stop them.

CHAPTER 12
AUGUST 26TH 1940

"I need to speak to you soon," Anna whispered to me as we connected the first set of tubes to the cattle. "But not while Robert's around." Robert had joined us for the milking, as he sometimes did. "After breakfast if that's okay." I nodded. I assumed this was something more to do with her affair with Charlie or the conflict with Robert and Susan. I was not really in talking mood. I felt about as gloomy as I had done when my father, Henri and I had driven away from my mother in Poland. I had looked back at her waving at us as long as I could, until the car had swept around a bend and she had disappeared from my sight. Was it some premonition, I wondered. Had something bad happened to Piotr, or to Roger? I'd found out nothing of any clarity in my reconnoitre the day before, except knowing again that the attacks had been sustained, damaging and deadly.

During breakfast the telephone rang. Robert answered it and I could hear him talking in the hallway where the telephone stood on a small table. Then he came back to the kitchen. "It's the Land Army," he said. "They want to know if I can spare one of you to go to North Weald and help to clear the village up. I said I could if one of you would go. They're holding the line."

It was obvious which of us would go. Anna knew about my friendship with the pilots, though I had not confided in her as she had in me. But we both knew that she and Charlie also enjoyed my being absent from the farm. Katherine showed no interest in being away from the farm. I think she had sensed that all was not well between Anna and Charlie, and still hoped for her opportunity with him.

"I'll go," I said, standing up quickly and brushing crumbs off my clothes. "I can cycle there. Tell them I'll go."

Robert completed the call and told me that I did not need to take any tools or equipment. The ARP wardens would provide all that. But I should expect to get dirty. They needed to clear up the buildings that had been bombed, and it would be hard, dirty work.

Susan quickly prepared some sandwiches for me, for which I was grateful. And she gave me a flask of tea, saying that I could drink it even when it went cold. It might be cleaner than any water I'd get in North Weald today.

Of course I was willing to help. But my ulterior motive was to find out, if possible, what had happened to Piotr and Roger, and whether they were safe. I cycled quickly down the side roads around Epping and then found myself on the same road as the day before. This time the roadblock consisted of an elderly woman, herself with a cycle. "Authorised Personnel only" read the sign that she had propped up on the road. I explained that I had been summoned by the Land Army to assist with clearing up the village, and she let me pass.

It was the first time since we left Poland that I had seen bomb damage. In the village many windows had been blown out, and householders were still fixing boards across the window spaces. But I was again struck, as I had been in Poland, by the stark contrast between the general housing and buildings, which had withstood the blast of the bombs that had fallen on the village, and the complete destruction of the buildings that had experienced the direct hits. They were no more than piles of bricks and debris, with their previous contents, whether domestic items or, in the case of the Post Office, the stationery and forms used by customers, strewn among the general chaos. The randomness of the bombs and of their consequences was starkly emphasised.

When I reached the village centre, which was near the airfield, I saw a lorry which the ARP had obviously set up as some sort of temporary HQ, and I reported there. They asked me to work on one of the houses that had been hit. Two people from the house had been killed, and they had removed the bodies, but they wanted to clear as much of the rubble away as they could to check that no other bodies were in the ruins. Two other people were working on the site when I reached it. One was a Land Girl whom I had never met before. Her name was Claire. She said that she was from Raines Hall, and that two or three others were also at work around the village. The other was one of the two ARP wardens who had stopped me on the road the day before. His name was Eric. He greeted me as if I were an old friend and explained that we had to clear the bricks and any intact roof tiles into piles at one side of the site, because they might be re-used in any re-building. But the wood, mortar, windows and glass, and any other items should be piled on the other side, and we had shovels and wheelbarrows to assist with this. Any items from the house itself, especially if it might be of any financial or sentimental value, should be kept separately. The ARP would remove and store them. Even in North Weald, he told me, there was a risk of looting.

As we worked I asked Claire if she knew Lewi. She said that she did, and that Lewi had volunteered to work on the bombed properties just as she had done. Miss Capthorn had not selected her as one of the Girls to go and do the work. Lewi had been quite upset and had been telling other Girls of her anger. She claimed Miss Capthorn knew she had reasons to want to go to the village but was deliberately ignoring them. I explained to Claire what I thought lay behind Lewi's anger, that she had wanted to see how the pilots were faring after the attack, and that she was friends with two of them, but not in any way romantically attached. Unlike me, I almost said. But that would have been a confidence too many for a first conversation.

Claire and I got on with the task in hand, picking out bricks and wheeling them to the growing piles that had already been started before my arrival. When we had picked out a couple of barrow loads, we would shovel in the loose debris, mortar and so on that remained and dump it on the piles as required. We found photographs, some broken furniture, crockery, a pair of spectacles in a case, some metal pots and the remains of a cooker. We dug the personal items out and stored them, and gradually some space started to grow in front of us. It was saddening us to think of a precious home such as this being suddenly and murderously devastated, and that quietened us. I suppose in both our minds was also the thought that there might be many more such ruined homes to be dug out in the weeks and months to come. Fear had been a dominant emotion of the previous five months, and seeing evidence of what one feared was no comfort. Quite the opposite in fact.

Eric said that he had received some training on managing the aftermath of attacks such as the one on North Weald. In some cases it would not be safe to attempt to clear a bombed building so readily, because the damaged property might collapse further. But since we could see as we cleared the debris where the floorboards and foundations of the building were, there was no risk of such a collapse. Also, the house did not have a cellar, which was why the two people inside had been killed. They had been cowering under the dining table, seeking shelter there, but the impact of a direct hit was too much. It was just as Robert had implied, I remembered. The table that Anna and I might shelter beneath would not protect us if the building was directly smashed down. Eric was retired from working in the City of London, he told us, and thought that working as a warden was an appropriate and helpful job to continue to do something useful. He was quite elderly, but sprightly, and he certainly put his heart into the work. He mostly left Claire and me to work together.

At around one o'clock, when we had cleared several yards of rubble away from the original house, Eric suggested that we should seek a cup of tea from the ARP lorry in the village. I took my sandwiches, and on the small village green I sat down with Claire and we talked about the various jobs we had done on our farms. I was able to explain more about Miss Capthorn's hostility towards Lewi and the reasons behind it. We both noticed that there were several visiting groups of men, some in uniform and some in suits, who arrived in cars or service vehicles. No doubt they were assessing the damage on the airfield and in the village. I also thought I saw Will's lorry drive through the village towards the airfield. I assumed he was delivering or picking up some agricultural items, and thought nothing more of it. We ended our lunch break by using the toilet facilities in the one remaining village pub, which had thrown open its doors to those helping to clear up the rubble, and we returned to work.

By four o'clock both Claire and I were flagging. Although used to working on the land, neither of us had done so much heavy lifting as we had done that day. Our arms, legs and backs were aching, we complained to one another. The piles of bricks and workable tiles were a testimony to our work, and the ARP lorry did indeed pick up all the personal items that we had plucked out of the debris. There was going to be a need for more days of labour to continue to clear up the damage. Eric thought another two days for three people. We both said that they might need to find other volunteers, though I don't think we really meant it. It felt like very important work, to show everyone who lived in the village or who came to see the damage that Hitler was not winning. I was however leaning on my spade, tired and sore, when I saw what I thought was Roger's car passing by. He was in the passenger seat. I cried out at the top of my voice for him but the car seemed to be going on ahead. I ran to the footpath and waved frantically. The car stopped, and Roger from the passenger seat looked back down the road, saw me and climbed out of the car. His right arm was in a sling. He waved and walked towards me, but he had a grim look on his face. I ran towards him. "What happened?" I gasped out, pointing at his arm.

"I broke it," he said. "Baling out of my plane. Landed in a tree and caught it on a branch. But…."

"But what?" I demanded. "What is it?" He did not answer, and I blurted out, "It's Piotr, isn't it?"

He nodded and guided me over to a bench that stood by the side of the house next door to the one I had been working on. "It is," he said, looking me straight in the eyes. "He was wounded yesterday. Fighting off the attack, as he did the day before as well. He got hit in the leg, and …." Again he tailed off.

"What, what?" I was shouting now.

"He stayed up there fighting, instead of coming down. He only landed when the bombers turned tail and ran home. By that time he'd lost a lot of blood. I don't know how he managed to land his kite so well. But he passed out as the ambulance got to him."

"Where is he? How is he?"

"He's in the hospital at Epping. Most of the casualties were moved there. In case there was another attack. They were due to operate today to remove the bullet. He was too weak last night."

I stiffened on hearing this. "He's alive but in danger! That's it, isn't it? I must go there."

"I'll take you there. I've got someone driving the car. I was coming to tell you. Didn't know you'd been here all along. This is the first I've been able to leave the airfield. We've had to oversee a lot of repair work, and it's still going on. Bloody Luftwaffe. Piotr tried to warn us all, didn't he? But no-one would listen to a Polish pilot. Perhaps they'll listen next time."

I grabbed my pullover, shouted a farewell to Claire and Eric and ran with Roger to the car and climbed in. The driver was another airman, whose plane had also been shot up but who had avoided injury. Roger said that the RAF was likely to bring in another squadron to North Weald because so many of the Hurricanes needed repairs. The airfield was still operational though and could put up some air defences if attacked again. But Roger thought that other airfields were perhaps more likely now to be the target. He said that in some ways it was good that Piotr was only wounded. The pilots who had been burned when the enemy shot through their fuel tanks were in a far worse state. I was not reassured. I felt angry that I had not been told about Piotr earlier, that I had worked all day so close to the airfield where people knew of his injury and admission to hospital. But I also knew that I would not be listed as a next of kin. The responsible officers would not have been under any obligation to inform me. Roger had been going out of his way to do so. That calmed me a little, but I was still almost rude in my farewell when we reached the hospital, so quickly did I run into the building to try to discover where Piotr was.

As it transpired, Piotr was still in an operating theatre when I arrived. Once the nurses had been assured that I was his fiancée (yes, I had to lie to get admittance) they told me that he had arrived the previous evening in a poor condition, having lost so much blood. They had stabilised him, and in the afternoon the doctors had decided it was time to operate on him to remove the bullet, which was deeply embedded near the bone in his thigh. It was a straightforward operation, but Piotr would be tired and woozy. He might not be in any state to talk, or perhaps even to recognise me. I told them that nevertheless I would stay to see him, and an hour later he was wheeled on a trolley back into the ward. The nurses provided me with a seat, and a lukewarm tea and dry scone which they said apologetically was the only food left on the ward. And I had to wait for Piotr to come around. His breathing seemed shallow to me, but it was steady. The evening drew on and beyond the windows of the ward it was growing dark. The nurses pulled blackout curtains across the windows so that they could turn some lights on. They checked regularly on Piotr and pointed out the other patients in the ward who had also been brought in the day previously. There were air crew, soldiers, and civilians. Several of them, like Piotr, had undergone operations, and the nurses had allowed two or three relatives to sit by beds as I had been allowed to. While I waited for Piotr to come round, I spoke to them, and we exchanged information about the patients we were watching. One or two of the combatants asked me about their comrades, but I had to confess to knowing little about such things. I did not want to be the one to tell them that there had been some significant losses.

Piotr's eyes eventually started to flutter a little, and the nurses told me that he was starting to regain consciousness. I was not to rush him, they said. Better if I just let him know I was there and that he was okay. So when his eyes opened I simply stood where he could see me, and whispered to him. He tried to smile, and he spoke my name. I took his hand in mine, and then sat down. After a while, he simply fell asleep. The nurse said that she did not think that he would wake again for some hours and suggested that I should go home. "Is that nearby?" she asked. I muttered that it was, but only as I walked along the corridor towards the exit did I realise that I had foolishly left my cycle in North Weald. I hesitated about what to do. It was a good two miles walk to where my cycle, I hoped, was still leaning against the remainder of the garden wall of the destroyed house. The farm was nearer, but if I walked there I would have no transport if I was called back to North Weald, or indeed to the hospital, for I had left the farm's telephone number with the nurse on Piotr's ward. I think my judgement must have been clouded, because I decided to walk back to collect the cycle and then to return on it to the farm.

If the forest was dark before, it now had an all-encompassing blackness that began to terrify me. I could walk along the road easily enough, listening out for any car that might be journeying without lights along the same road, but the silence of the forest, broken occasionally by the sound of animals within the darkness, began to work on my imagination. After a few hundred yards I started to hear a noise from within the forest that was more than an owl hooting or a fox hunting. It sounded like footsteps, running through the forest and drawing nearer to me. I stopped in anguish. It was too late to turn back to Epping. And I was reluctant to burst into a run on such a dark and potentially dangerous surface as this country lane. I stood still, dreading whatever was approaching, when suddenly two large running creatures almost brushed against me. I screamed, and fell, and they swerved away from me. Hooves clattered on the tarmac of the road. I realised they were deer, probably a mother and fawn. Deer roamed the forest there, though one only rarely saw them. At night they ventured out more widely than during the day, when they usually remained deep in the forest gloom. I lay on the ground for a few moments. Part of me just wanted to continue lying there, but the better part of me – yes there is somewhere within me a better part – urged me to get up and get on with what I needed to do, which I did. I stood up, brushed myself down a little, and marched on through the forest. I was angry, exhausted, lonely but determined. I was not going to give way to all the things that seemed to have gone wrong for me.

In North Weald itself some work was still going on within the airfield. There were noises of hammering and screeching of metal being shaped or cut for some purpose. But the village itself was quiet and dark. The ARP lorry was still there and I guessed that some of the wardens might be sleeping within its covered back and platform. No-one seemed to see me as I went off to find my cycle, which had not been moved from its spot, and certainly nobody challenged me. I rode slowly and carefully out of the village and found my way back to the farm with the help of a little moonlight, the moon having come up just in time to assist me. Once or twice I found myself almost falling asleep as I cycled, and I almost fell off. I was so tired, my body ached, and I was very dispirited.

I dismounted outside the farm, not wanting to make any noise to wake either those in the farmhouse or Anna. I wheeled the cycle through the gap at the side of the house and leaned it against the barn. It was not where I usually stored it, but it was so late and so dark that I did not want to delay myself by securing it inside the barn. When I stepped away from the barn I tripped over something large and quite heavy on the ground. As I tried to get up,

I realised that it was a person lying there. And feeling the rough material of the person's clothes, I knew it was a Land Army uniform, and that this was Anna, not Katherine. And although I instantly knew there was no hope, I hissed loudly, "Anna, Anna, wake up," and I shook her violently. But she did not move. So I screamed. I screamed for Anna. I screamed for Piotr. I screamed for myself. I screamed until they came to find out what had happened.

CHAPTER 13
AUGUST 27TH-28TH 1940

I sat sobbing in the kitchen for an hour or so. Robert called the emergency services, but once they'd established that Anna was dead, and that no intruder was suspected, they took their time in arriving. Susan gave up waiting for them and half-dragged me across the yard, well away from where they had covered Anna's body with a blanket, and got me to my bed. I fell asleep in my clothes, and I think Susan sat in our living room until the ambulance came. I must have been feverish, because when I woke up Susan tried to force some medicine on me, but I wouldn't take it. When I asked what was happening, she told me that the ambulance had come and taken Anna away, and that there were two policemen checking where Anna had fallen. She seemed to have been in the barn, and to have fallen out of the opening in the loft where we had worked the pulley to haul sacks up for storage just weeks ago. No-one knew exactly what had happened, but the policemen were calling it an accident.

I jumped up on hearing that, pulled my boots on – I still had my clothes on from the day before, all dusty and begrimed from clearing rubble – and ran out into the yard. Sure enough two uniformed officers were measuring the distance from the barn to the outline of Anna's body that someone had chalked on the floor of the yard. They were noting the distance in one of their notebooks. I accosted them before they went inside the barn.

"She was scared of heights," I blurted out. "Anna, Anna suffered from vertigo. She wouldn't have gone near the edge of the platform up there. She was terrified of it!"

The policemen stopped and looked at me suspiciously. I must have looked a strange sight, my clothing filthy, my hair all tousled where I'd been asleep, and my face streaked by the tears I had shed. "Sorry, miss, I don't understand. Are you," he looked at his notebook, "Miss Beauchamp? You found the body of Anna, I believe." Again he looked at his notebook.

"Yes, yes, that's right. And I don't think she would have just fallen from the opening up there. She would never go near it. I know that because I worked with her up there."

"But what else could have happened to her?" the other policeman asked. He sounded a little more aggressive than his partner. I said nothing, though my thoughts were racing in my head. What indeed could have happened to her? Might she have gone up there to meet Charlie? Did they have a row? Or did Robert or Susan find her up there and argue with her about her affair with their son? Or did Katherine know that she was up there and fight with her, or even take the opportunity to get rid of her rival?

"Are you saying that she might have killed herself, miss?" The policeman looked at me as if I were a fool. "There's no reason to think that, is there?" I was silent. I had not for a moment thought that. The Anna that I had first met when I arrived at the farm was upset, made distraught by the tension around her relationship with Charlie. One might I suppose have believed in a suicide then. And things had not gone well when she and Charlie…. But she was still determined to be with him, believing that it would come right. I could not tell the policemen what I knew of that. I did not think she might have killed herself. But if they were concluding that her death was just some unfortunate accident, I could not accept that either.

Susan had followed behind me. Now she took my arm and offered me tea and something to eat in the kitchen. "The milking? Who's to do the milking?" I asked.

"Robert and Katherine can do that," Susan said, and as we approached the door into the farmhouse, Robert came out in boots and the apron that he usually wore when he helped with the milking. "We're all at sixes and sevens," Susan said to me. "Charlie won't come down from his room. Robert is angry because of that and because of what's happened. And we're all upset about Anna. I don't know what to think. But I know you need some food and drink and then you can tidy yourself up. The police are likely to need a statement from you, and you won't want to go to the police station looking like you do."

"Did you stay with me last night?" I asked.

"Yes, I dozed the night away in the armchair. I was worried about you. You were talking about the attack on the airfield and about the hospital and about walking through the forest and being scared by two deer. I didn't understand you but I could see how upset you were."

"They're all things that happened to me before I got back last night. Before I found Anna." I jumped up as if I were about to go out to the yard, as if I wanted to confirm that this was not all some bad dream that had been visited upon me."

"Sit still," Susan said, gently guiding me back to my seat. "It was awful, for you and for all of us. I didn't think I would stop you screaming. I was angry with Anna, I won't deny that, but I wouldn't have wished this upon her ever. No-one deserves to die like that." I accepted that I should stay silent now. I had suspicions but at that point I was not willing to share them any further. If I had to go up to the police station in Epping to make a statement, I would raise them then.

The policemen looked in on Susan and me before they left. They asked me to make a statement at the station, and I thought that at least I would be able to visit Piotr after doing so. Susan suggested that I should take a bath and refresh myself, and I agreed that it would be a good idea. I wanted to make the right impression when I went to the police station.

It was around lunchtime, therefore, when I entered the tall building that stood in the middle of the High Street. But when I was asked to take a seat and wait for someone to take my statement, and then when after an hour no-one had even so much as glanced at me, let alone invited me in to talk about Anna, I started to become gloomy. It did not seem that anybody had any doubts or questions about what had happened; there was no urgency about any investigation; and given that the emergency services had probably been overwhelmed with work following the attacks at the airfield, nobody seemed bothered at all to talk to me. "Should I come back later?" I asked the man at the desk at the front entrance. He assured me that the policemen involved in Anna's case would come to see me soon, but it was another half hour before one of the two uniformed men who had been at the farm earlier summoned me through to a bare, poorly furnished room with a table, two chairs and a dilapidated typewriter.

The officer looked at me for a short while. I hope he thought that I had scrubbed up rather well compared with my appearance in the night. I had bathed, washed my hair, done my make-up, put some civilian clothes on while Susan took my uniform off to wash it, and generally tried to make an impression. "We just need a short statement from you about how you found the body in the yard of the farm, what time it was, at least approximately, and what you did then," he said. It was as if he were putting words in my mouth.

"I want to say a little more than that," I said. He looked a little disconsolate at that and asked me why. "Because I don't believe that Anna would ever willingly have gone near the opening in the loft of the barn. She suffered from vertigo. It would have terrified her if she had."

"Well maybe that's what happened," he countered. "Perhaps she became dizzy and fell as a result of that." He paused. Looked at me again for a few seconds. "Look, we know from the family there that the young woman was having some kind of an affair with young Charlie, the son. His mother told us that. And that she thought they sometimes met up in that loft. Perhaps she was waiting for him. Perhaps he didn't show up and she went to the edge to look for him. We will take a statement from him, about when he last saw her and if he knew of any reason why she would be in the loft."

"Did Susan or Robert tell you about all the conflict and arguments there have been at the farm?" I asked. "Arguments about this affair between them. Involving both the parents, and the other Land Girl?"

"No they didn't. But it's not really surprising, is it? I'm sure your parents would have some kind of view about any man you were walking out with. There's nothing unusual in that."

I had to concede that he had a point. I had deliberately not told my father about how strongly Piotr felt about me, nor about the small ways in which I could feel myself reciprocating. He would have been concerned, for sure, about the vulnerability of a Hurricane pilot stationed in

Essex at that time. He would have wanted to discourage me, I thought. My mother – what would she have thought? She'd have liked the fact that he was Polish, and that he was fighting the enemy. She would probably have encouraged me, I thought. There in a nutshell was my dilemma.

"Miss," he said. I'd obviously been momentarily lost in my thoughts. "Is everything all right? Can you make your statement now?"

It took a while to complete the document. His typing skills seemed to be no better than mine might have been, and he had to use correcting fluid several times to ensure its accuracy. I did manage to mention how long I'd worked with Anna, and that she had been caught up in conflict with members of the family because of a developing friendship with Charlie, but that she had seemed much happier in recent weeks. Also that I knew that she suffered from vertigo, from working with her in the loft. Then I described encountering her body in the yard, and how I'd screamed for help. He didn't want to put all this into the statement and tried arguing with me. He even said again that I was risking making my friend's accidental death look like a possible suicide. But I insisted.

Something about Anna's death was not right, I was sure of it. I'd seen her reaction that morning in the loft. There was no way that she would ever have approached the opening. And she was not suicidal – quite the opposite. I thought that she had come to harm because of another person, but I did not put that in my statement, or say it to the officer.

I thought they would dismiss the whole statement if I did that. I would have to pursue that thought myself.

I walked to the end of the High Street and beyond, to where the road forked off for North Weald and the hospital. I wanted to see how Piotr was doing, and I found that he was a little recovered, by which I mean that he was awake and able to smile when he saw me. I sat down, took his hand, and asked how he was. He tried to answer but his voice was weak, and I could hardly hear it. I moved my ear closer to his lips, and he whispered that he was feeling a little better, but still weak. He couldn't sit up yet, but somehow he managed to lift his head and kiss the side of my neck. He sank back down again. I stroked his face and smiled at him. I said I was pleased to see him recovering. I did not mention Anna. That could wait. But I wanted to speak to a nurse so I walked to the front of the ward where there was a small reception desk. I asked the nurse on duty about Piotr, and she said he was recovering slowly. It had been very touch-and-go when he came in, she reported, looking at his notes. It would take quite a while for him to get fully better, but the wound was healing satisfactorily and the operation had been a success. The doctors had removed a bullet that would otherwise have caused him great difficulty. I asked if he would stay in the hospital. She could not answer that. It depended on the hospital authorities and the RAF. If they had room in one of the RAF-designated hospitals, they might move him there, but she thought that with so much fighting, and so many RAF personnel injured and wounded, it might not be possible to find a bed. In which case Piotr would stay in the hospital, at least until he could be moved to a nursing unit somewhere for convalescence.

I sat with him for a while longer, made small talk with him, though it was mostly me talking and him listening, and held his hand throughout. He wanted to stroke my arm, to run his fingers through my hair, and I allowed him to do it, finding that I enjoyed the physical sensation. And if I did, I thought, how much more so would he, who had so recently flirted with death rather than with me.

After a while he seemed to tire, and I thought he was going to sleep. I stood up, apologised that I had to leave, and promised to come again as soon as I could. I leaned over him and kissed him on the lips. He smiled once more and asked me to kiss him again. I did so, and he immediately made it more passionate, and I felt his tongue collide with mine and caress it. Even in such a weakened state, his desire was obvious. I told him playfully not to be so bold, in a hospital especially. We should be more decorous. But he showed his disapproval of that approach.

Outside the hospital it had started to rain. I sought some shelter in a tea room and tried to gather my thoughts. Anna first. If she had been killed, as I thought was quite possible, who would have done it? A few weeks ago I'd have thought any of the family there might have done so. Charlie was pressing her to go all the way with him and they had indeed had a brief but unsuccessful encounter – he might have done it in temper if they'd had a row, for example if she'd refused him this time. Either of his parents might have had an argument with her if they'd seen her going up there. They'd have guessed she was meeting Charlie. That could have led to a fight, and a tragic conclusion. But there had been much less conflict in recent weeks. Robert and Susan seemed almost to have accepted the situation, though I did not know if they were aware of how advanced the relationship was. Perhaps, though it seemed unlikely to me, Katherine had followed Anna and they had an argument about Charlie in the loft. But I could not fully believe any of the four was a murderer. None of the conflicts or arguments I had witnessed or heard about had suggested that level of violence was present. It did not make sense.

And then there was Piotr. I felt for him, but what did I feel? Admiration, for what he was doing, in a country not his own? Pity, for the danger he was placing himself in daily, and now for the almost deadly wound he had suffered? Friendship – he was good company, kind, considerate, gentle, respectful? But love? I still did not know. My mother had once said that when it's love, you can't imagine life without the person you love. You can't imagine that person leaving you, for ever. Life without them is unimaginable. And yet she had stayed in Poland, had in effect left both my father and me. But I knew she did not want that to be for ever. And her refusal to leave did not mean an end of love. It meant that her sense of duty was so strong that at the time it had outweighed her love for us. Just as Piotr's sense of duty drove him to stay fighting in the air even when he was wounded and should have been landing his plane. But I could not love him out of a sense of duty. It had to be as my mother had said – my life had to be unimaginable if it was without him. Then I would know it was love.

I arrived back at the farm in time to change into my laundered uniform and help with the milking. It was a distraction at least to be doing something when my thoughts were so troubled. Robert helped me to bring the cattle in. He did not talk about Anna. In fact he did not talk to me about anything. I guessed that in his own way he was as troubled as I was. Katherine had asked for a day off after the traumatic events and had gone to visit her family. She was not expected back until the afternoon of the next day. Over dinner I heard that Charlie had gone into Epping to make his statement to the police, and Susan guessed he'd probably gone on to drown his sorrows in one of the pubs on the High Street. Unhappiness had settled over all of us, so I went to bed early, and after some tossing and turning, managed to fall asleep. I felt that Anna's ghost was sleeping in the bed alongside mine.

Next morning Robert again helped me with the milking. He said he was worried about the Land Army. He thought he still needed another Land Girl. The harvest was imminent, and there was a lot of labour required in the fields. The five of us might manage it if Susan joined in, but she had not done much farm work for some years. He thought the Land Army might not send another Girl. After all, one had left complaining about the atmosphere at the farm, and now another one had died in the yard. The Army might not want to send anyone, and any Girl who found out about what had happened might run a mile rather than join such a troubled farm. If he was looking for my opinion on this, I couldn't give it. The thoughts and ways of the Land Army were a bit of a mystery to me, and I did not know how they might decide in a case like Robert's. I muttered something about telling the Army that the harvest was vital and would be in jeopardy without more help. But I could not reassure him. I had my own doubts about events, after all. I wasn't even sure of my own safety, especially if I raised my doubts about Anna's death.

After the milking was complete, and breakfast was over, Robert asked me to do some hedging work on one of the perimeter fields. I raised my eyebrows because this was normally Charlie's work. He looked after all the fences and hedges of the farm, being responsible for the security of the herd. But Robert said that he did not think that Charlie was in any fit state to do any work today, and the hedges that he was directing me towards were starting to encroach on the lane beyond the field. People would be complaining soon if we didn't do something about it. So I took the hedging tools, picked up the sandwich that Susan had made for me, filled my bottle of water and set off for the walk to the edge of the farm. When I reached the hedge that Robert wanted me to cut I could see that he was right. The hedge was sagging and leaning over the lane, which had no separate path or paving. A large vehicle, a lorry or bus for example, would brush against it. I had to find the gate into the lane, climb over the stile, and start to cut the overgrowing branches. These I had to fling back over the hedge into the field. If I left them where they fell Robert would find people complaining about that. I wondered if Charlie had been similarly neglectful of other parts of the farm's perimeter. It would add to Robert's difficulties if he had.

I had to work hard to start to bring order back to the stretch of hedge. Sometimes I was on tiptoe trying to reach the branches that were in the middle of the hedge, and sometimes despite my best efforts the branches that I threw landed on the hedge rather than on the other side. The physical effort reminded me why this work was normally left to Charlie. But it was quiet there. Only a very occasional car came down the lane, and no-one stopped to talk. So I was surprised at around midday when Charlie himself suddenly accosted me from the other side of the hedge.

"I need to talk to you," he said. His tone was surly.

"Come down to the gate then," I replied. "We can't really talk over the hedge. I can't easily see you."

We met across the gate therefore. He looked still hungover from the night before, his skin rather sallow and his eyes a little bloodshot. I couldn't help my reaction showing him I was aware of his condition.

"I'm sorry," I said, "so sorry about Anna. It must be terrible for you. She was so pretty. I know you loved each other. I can't stop thinking about her." My words seemed, at least initially, to soften his mood.

"You're right," he said. "She was pretty, and I was in love with her. And she was in love with me. We'd even talked about getting married, though mum and dad were completely opposed to her."

"I know they were. I couldn't help knowing that."

"But that's why I want to talk to you. I went up to the police station. They said you'd told them about all the arguing that had gone on. They questioned me about it. Made me feel really uncomfortable, talking about such personal things. It was none of your business. Why did you tell them about it?"

I felt quite uncomfortable about this. We were in an isolated spot. I had only mentioned the conflict in the family because I did not believe that Anna's death was accidental. It was right, therefore that the police had questioned Charlie. But I had not anticipated him then coming to question me about it. "I'm not sure," I said slowly. "I just thought it was some background that they needed to know about."

"But why? It's private. It's only about us. They don't need to know. And they also said you'd told them Anna suffered from vertigo. Why did you do that?"

I realised I'd been fairly dim to think that what I told the police would not be repeated back to Charlie. I'd left myself exposed to him by what I'd said. And if by some chance he had killed Anna, he was now aware of my suspicions. "I just thought it was odd, that she'd fallen from somewhere she was so scared of. She told me she suffered from vertigo."

"It never stopped her from going up there with me." His protest made me feel even more uncomfortable. Charlie had hardly ever spoken to me before. His attention had always been focussed on Anna, and on being with her. Now he was admitting that he had met her in the secrecy of the loft. I wasn't sure if that suggested innocence or guilt on his part, but it was certainly a big departure from any previous conversation we had held.

"Charlie, I know you're very upset. I was upset when I found Anna. I've only said to the police what I thought I should tell them. We both need some time and space to get over it. You look a bit jaded after yesterday. Why don't you go back to the farm now? I don't think we have anything more to say to one another right now."

"I'll say this before I go. I loved Anna. She was the best thing that ever happened to me, and I don't want you spoiling my memory of her. So keep your nose out of our affairs. You're just a Land Girl, not a bloody detective!" He turned and walked off, leaving me troubled by his visit and what he had said. I realised that I was shaking. From anger? Fear? Anguish? Probably from all three.

CHAPTER 14
AUGUST 28TH 1940

I finished the hedging work as best I could. I had been upset by the argument with Charlie, but I was still determined that I would not accept that Anna had simply fallen from the winching platform. I left all the cuttings on the ground inside the hedge. Robert, perhaps with me accompanying him, would have to come out tomorrow with the tractor, and either burn them in the corner of the field or bring them back to the farm to cut up and add to the large compost piles which were around the back of the barn. My walk back to the Farm was more of a trudge. I was tired by the work, and by all that had happened, and I felt unhappy and anxious. I stored the tools in the barn, and found that Susan had come out of the house to talk to me.

"We've heard from the police," she said. "They've completed their investigation and reported to the coroner that Anna died as a result of an accidental fall in the dark.

The coroner has accepted that and is not going to ask for a post-mortem or an inquest. So Anna's parents have decided that the funeral will be on Friday. The funeral directors are in Romford. Apparently family and friends can visit from three o'clock today until five o'clock tomorrow. Charlie's going to visit this evening. I'm not sure what Robert and I will do."

This all came out in a rush, so that it was hard for me to absorb all the information. Susan was obviously looking at me to see how I reacted. I could have exploded. I could have used every swearword I know, English, French and Polish, to describe those lazy policemen and their indolent coroner. I could have screamed as I had done when lying on the floor with Anna's dead body. But if there had been foul play in her death, screaming, shouting and swearing would not help me in unravelling what had occurred. I needed to stay calm.

"I'm surprised it's all happened so quickly," I said as coolly as I could. "I thought it would take longer."

"I suppose with all that's happened at the airfield they're all busy. They probably just want to get this death over with."

"Yes, I can understand that." I was thinking about what I should do. It was clearly no use going to talk to the police again. What could I say to change their minds? It occurred to me, however, that I had not really seen Anna fully after I discovered her dead body. Yes in the dark I had recognised her, but more by her clothing than by her face, which was almost invisible to me. "I think I'd like to visit her, to see her, at the funeral directors."

"Are you sure? It can be quite upsetting, you know. Looking at a dead body is not for everyone."

"Yes I would. I could cycle over there if you tell me where to go. I think it would help me to recover after her...." I did not really think this. I knew I would in fact find it very upsetting, to see the dead body of someone I had watched coming to life fully as a woman, in those few weeks I had known her, and to see her beauty – because she had been beautiful – destroyed. I would be very upset. But it might, it just might, help me to work out what had happened to her.

"I'll write the details down for you. Have you seen Charlie at all?"

"Yes, he came out to talk to me." Susan was clearly surprised by this. "He wanted to talk to me about Anna." I paused. I would need at some time to raise these matters with Susan, so I pressed on. "It was because I had told the police there had been some conflict here involving Anna, and I'd told them that she suffered from vertigo."

Susan's demeanour changed. Since I had discovered Anna, she had been considerate and thoughtful towards me, even kind. Now she challenged me. "Why did you tell them that? I thought they just wanted a statement about how you found her. Some of what you've told them is personal about us. Was Charlie upset about what you'd said?" The questions came at me like machine-gun fire. It was interesting how both she and Charlie had taken umbrage at what I'd put in my statement.

"Yes, he was upset because he thought that what I'd put down was private. But I thought it might be relevant. I did not know that the police would tell him what I'd written down." I should have known, of course, or at least I should have thought about it. I should have checked with the policeman taking my statement what he was going to do with it. I should have asked him not to tell Charlie that it was I who had said these things. But once again I was too dim to have thought about it. I know it's silly, but even at that point in my conversation with Susan, when she was smarting with indignation, I wondered to myself when I would stop being so dim. Or even if I would ever stop. I seemed to have a unique habit of rubbing people up the wrong way because I had acted stupidly!

Susan asked me why I had thought this information might be relevant. I steeled myself for what might be an explosive reaction, and said, "I'm not sure about how Anna died. Something seems wrong to me. She would never have gone near that winching platform, not near enough for her to fall. She was too frightened of it."

"So you think what? That she ran at it and jumped? That would be suicide. Is that what you want to be thought about her? The police made a point of saying to us that it was not suicide."

"I don't know," I said. I felt on the defensive. It was the second time someone had interpreted my statement as suggesting suicide. I had not intended that at all. But neither the police nor Susan now seemed able to draw the obvious inference. "I would like to see her, one last time."

I made clear that the conversation was over. Susan was evidently not happy. She turned on her heel and marched back to the house. I watched her, feeling disconsolate.

I went for a wash to clean myself up from the hedging. I decided to skip dinner and go to visit Piotr. I looked in at the house to tell Susan I would not want dinner because I was going to the hospital. She registered this but said nothing. The evening was cloudy but dry. It was good for cycling, and despite my arms being tired from the hedging, my legs were fine and I sped through Epping and up to the hospital in good time for visiting. I walked into the ward but was shocked when I reached Piotr's bed. It was empty, completely empty. There were new bedclothes and linen, all neatly turned down. The bedside cabinet, which had held a jug and glass of water for him, was empty. It was as if he had never been there. What had happened? My thoughts turned immediately to the worst. Had Piotr died, with no-one there to comfort him in his last moments? I stood there, frozen by my fears. Fortunately a nurse had seen my look of horror. She came over and took my arm and led me to a chair. She had recognised me from my previous visit, she said. She knew I was – she had hesitated here – close to him. He had taken a turn for the worse, she said. It was not unusual in such cases. She was sure he would recover. But he had been transferred to a larger hospital, Whipps Cross, near Leytonstone. They would be able to care for him better there.

"But nobody told me, nobody called to say where he was going," I protested.

"There are no next-of-kin details on his service cards. They bring them in when an airman or a soldier gets wounded. So nobody knew who to call. I am sorry."

There was nothing I could do. Leytonstone was a long cycle ride away, too far to go at that time of the evening. I could not see him. I could not find out what "taking a turn for the worse" meant. He would not receive any visitors. I could have cried. I almost did, I think. But once again, it would have been no use my doing so. The elements that were controlling us would not change. Piotr and I were the victims of the war, of our situations, of others' decisions. I could only try to engage with what lay in front of me, and most of all that was the mystery surrounding Anna's death.

I returned to the farm much more slowly on my cycle. As I moved along Epping High Street I briefly toyed with continuing in that direction, which would eventually bring me to Leytonstone and the new hospital. But I could already see the evening dark starting to fall. Visiting hours would be over before I reached the hospital, and my trip would then be completely in vain. Better, if I could, to try to get there next day.

Susan was obviously looking out for me when I returned to the farm. She asked me to come into the kitchen and talk to her and Robert. What now, I wondered, because I had not anticipated any more upsets that evening. I was near the end of my tether.

Susan invited me to sit at the table. Robert was already seated there. She spoke first. "We know you're upset by what has happened. We know you were friendly with

Anna. No-one would have wished for what has happened, nor that you should discover her lying there. We are sorry that it has all happened. But we want to ask you to stop suggesting that something suspicious has happened. The things you said to the police have really upset Charlie. He went to see Anna's body, and when he came back he said he had decided to join up as soon as possible. We hope we can persuade him to wait. The harvesting needs to be done and everything gathered in or sold. Without him it would be impossible. It's going to be hard enough as it is. Robert is worried that we won't get any more Land Girls. WarAg is telling us that we must plough up a lot more land, and plant vegetables. We can't manage if Charlie goes, and we can barely manage with just you and Katherine. If you keep on saying things about us, it will be even worse for us."

It was a long speech, and I could understand all that lay behind it. Charlie's hopes had been crushed, and if his feelings for Anna were anything like mine seemed to be concerning Piotr, he himself must feel destroyed. He might well react by giving up his protected status and taking himself off to the war. And the farm would indeed then be in jeopardy. The whole reason the government had formed the Land Army was that there was insufficient labour to run the farms. Robert and Susan could not do it on their own. But I was still determined to get justice for Anna. If someone had killed her, and it was not an accident, I wanted to find that out.

"I understand your worries," I tried to speak sympathetically, though I could feel my own tears waiting to burst out. "I don't want to cause you any unnecessary concern, but I am myself very worried that Anna may have been killed by someone, and that it was not an accident. I won't say anything more about it for the moment, but if I find anything else out, I will take it up again. It's only fair to Anna." Susan looked at Robert. He thought for a few moments, then nodded to her. They'd obviously decided to let her do the talking.

"Alright, we'll accept that," she said. "But we are sure that there was no-one here who would have killed Anna. There's no-one who would have wanted to. The police and the coroner agree. You can't really think that you know better than them."

It was hard to answer that. It was just that after the aversion she had shown when we were working in the loft, I was simply convinced that Anna could not have approached the opening in such a way that she fell. But I did not have any evidence of what the police call foul play, nor any real suspect. I shrugged. "I'm just very uneasy about it. Something seems wrong. That's all I can say." We accepted that our parley was over. Susan offered me some bread and cheese, since I hadn't eaten, which I accepted. Robert took himself off. I sensed that he was simmering inside but had resolved not to burst out in temper. His farm and livelihood were on a knife edge. He was controlling himself to save them, in his view.

CHAPTER 15

AUGUST 29TH 1940

Next morning Robert and Katherine helped me with the milking. He kept his conversation to the functional instructions and requests that any three people doing the milking would have shared. I thought it best not to try to widen the conversation. After breakfast I confirmed that I wanted to visit the undertaker's parlour. Susan looked concerned, but she gave me the sandwich which she had prepared for me anyway. I put it in the basket of my cycle, and also stuffed my mackintosh and hat into the basket. It looked as if it might rain. I had not told Susan and Robert but I hoped to visit Whipps Cross as well as the undertaker's. I'd worked out that if I could persuade the guard to transport my cycle, I could cover a large part of the journey from Romford to the hospital by train. Otherwise I was going to have to cycle much further than I had yet managed.

I had to ask my way several times on my journey to Romford. Travelling was not easy in areas one was unfamiliar with, because there were no signposts, no village signs, and all mention of locations had been removed from the roadside. The Land Army uniform helped me. People recognised it now, and obviously assumed that I was not familiar with the locality, having been transported from some urban life in which it was never necessary to know one's way. Unfortunately it did start to rain. My mackintosh gave some protection to my body but not to my legs. I could soon feel the wet soaking through my breeches, and I could not keep my hat on when the wind that accompanied the rain caught it. I put it back in the basket and accepted that I would be soaked.

It must have taken me an hour and a half to reach the undertakers. No doubt a better cyclist would have covered the distance much more quickly, but I was grateful to have the cycle to manage the journey. The trains from Epping were becoming more intermittent by the day as fuel shortages were affecting all transport. I might have taken well over two hours by using the train system. The undertaker's itself was a nondescript shop on the edge of the High Street. Purple velvet curtains hung from the edges of the window, and a small plaque gave the name of the owner and his profession. It also indicated that there was a chapel of rest. I entered the dark premises, and a stooping, aged fellow stood up. His hair was combed across his head in one of those male swirls that was intended to conceal his balding pate, and he peered at me through a pair of glasses that must have been Victorian in origin. Probably early Victorian!

"How can I help you?" he asked, his tone suggesting that he did not want to help me at all.

"I've come to see Anna," I whispered. I wasn't sure whether or not my request would be accepted, so I tried to indicate my weakness and sorrow. "Anna, my friend."

"I'm afraid only close relatives and those in a relationship with the deceased are allowed to visit her. Her parents' instructions. She was…er…damaged in a fall, you know."

I had feared there might be an obstacle. "Yes, I do know. It was I who found her. We were Land Girls together. I didn't want that to be my last memory of her." I started to cry, dabbing my eyes with a handkerchief. I felt a complete fraud. I had cried enough times genuinely in recent days, and had felt like crying even more often, yet now I had to put it on to deceive this black-clad gatekeeper. He was obviously thinking, and then he spoke. "I suppose if that's the case there can be no harm in it."

He led me down the corridor that ran through the premises. It became ever more gloomy with each step. He opened a final door, and there was the chapel of rest. A table contained a silver crucifix and two candles, which were lit and provided the only light. The back window was curtained shut. There was an overwhelmingly powerful sweet smell, a chemical smell, not a pleasant one. Anna's body was in a casket on a long, low table. Only the upper half was open, and Anna's pallid face was visible, surrounded by some white shrouding material that I guessed hid whatever blow on the head she had suffered through her fall. I gasped. Her face, even now four days after her death, showed some bruising around her mouth and her cheeks. I'm no pathologist, but I instantly knew that this bruising was not from her fall. If she had hit her face on the hard ground of the yard, there would have been brutal marking and cuts. Someone had held her tightly around the mouth, it was evident. I could almost make out the finger marks of the assailant. I tried to cover up my reaction by asking if I could sit for a while. The undertaker pulled over a chair that had been by the wall, and he placed it next to the casket. I sat and looked up at him tearfully. "Could I ask two things of you?" He nodded and gave a little bow. The atmosphere of the place seemed to reduce us both to whispers and to the utmost respect. "Could I just sit here alone with her for a while? And could I, could I, hold her hand? I never got to do it the night she died."

"It's most unusual," he said coldly. I dabbed my eyes a couple of times more. "Oh, very well. Just for five minutes. I can't give you more time." He leant over the casket and pulled the shroud back from Anna's body. Then he lifted her limp arm and gave me her hand. It was cold. I shuddered.

"Thank you," I again whispered, again showing him my teary face. "I'm very grateful."

The moment he left and had shut the door, I put Anna's hand temporarily on her body. I stood up and crossed the room and pulled the curtains back. It was a dingy back yard that I briefly saw, and it was still raining. I hurried back to Anna and quickly rolled up the sleeve of the blouse in which she had been dressed. There! There it was! The same tell-tale bruising on her arm as on her face, which now seemed to me to show its evidence of an assault on her even more clearly. One hand had covered her mouth, I guessed, and one had gripped her tightly. I quickly rolled the sleeve back down, again crossed the room and drew the curtains shut. I could have seen very little without the daylight in that sad room. I remained sitting, holding Anna's hand, until the undertaker came in. He took Anna's arm from me and, with a gentleness that I observed but had not expected, laid the arm back in the cocoon of the shroud, which he wrapped around her body once more. I stood, and I leaned over her body. I kissed her on the bruised cheek, and silently promised to do more to find out who had attacked her. I was now positive that she had been harmed, and that her death was no accident. There had not been a post-mortem examination, and the coroner had not looked at her at all. But I did not know what I could do about my certainty.

I managed to persuade a guard on the train at Romford Station to accept my cycle, explaining that I was visiting an RAF pilot who was seriously ill. Once again I made copious use of my handkerchief and the tears that were now ever ready to pour from my eyes. He relented, and I was able to sit thinking in a carriage as the Essex countryside gave way to the London suburbs outside the window. Even though I was sure that Anna had been killed, no-one in a position of authority was prepared to countenance the idea. I pondered the people with some power to intervene or take the matter up – the police, the coroner, the Land Army, Anna's parents. And I recognised that the only evidence that existed of the assault, the bruising on Anna's face and arms, would disappear next day when her funeral had taken place. I dismissed the Land Army because they would surely never listen to anything I said. I did not know where the coroner's offices were and could not see how I could find out in sufficient time to visit and persuade him to re-open the case. Anna's parents – I did not know where they lived, what they were like, nor how they might react if suddenly told that their daughter might have been murdered. That left only the police, whose location I knew, but whose intransigence I had already experienced. Despite that, the police it would have to be.

I found my way from Forest Gate station to the hospital only slowly. It was still raining, and I had hardly dried out from my earlier journey to Romford. I had to keep stopping to check with people on the streets that I was going in the right direction. Easy in Forest Gate itself, but not so simple when I crossed the wide open space of grass and forest land between there and Leytonstone, which one of the people I accosted simply called the Flats. Having found my way to the hospital itself, I was in some awe of the vast brick building that confronted me. Even more so inside the building. Reception staff directed me to a ward at the other end of the building. "It's a long walk," they said. It certainly was. At regular intervals off the corridor there were wards stretching away at right angles, and there were wards on top of those wards. Dozens of them. And dozens of people walking along the corridor, each with their own concerns and anxieties, probably much like mine about Piotr. Few, I thought, would be harbouring thoughts about a possible murder. More likely they shared the general fear of bombing or invasion that had gripped us all in recent weeks and months.

I was shocked to see Piotr. His decline was all too obvious. He was lying unconscious in his bed, sweat evident on his face, and he moved his head from side to side every few minutes as if trying to shake off the infection that was raging within him. To gain access I had to tell the nurses I was his fiancée – I again did not think girlfriend would suffice – and they complained that it was not mentioned on his records. "No, his proposal was quite recent," I said, wondering if I would have to reach for my handkerchief yet again. They relented and led me to his bedside. I asked if I could dry his face, and they provided a facecloth and a towel. I could feel his high temperature when my hand touched his forehead. He did not wake, but he seemed to respond to the towelling. I was deeply worried. I knew that infections from wounds were the third-greatest fear of the pilots (the first was death itself, and the second was being burned). Blood-poisoning it was often called. My father often said it killed as many soldiers on the Western Front as the bullets and shells themselves had done. Piotr had a bad case of it, that was evident. I sat there for perhaps an hour, towelling his face and hands dry several times. The nurses did not interrupt me. They were probably grateful to have someone doing it instead of them. Eventually a doctor appeared at the bedside. "Who are you?" he asked. I explained again that I was Piotr's fiancée, of recent event, and asked him about Piotr. "It's not good at the moment," he said, "his infection is bad and his body has not managed to fight it off. The next day or two will decide, we think. I'm sorry I can't say any better than that."

"I'm grateful to you for being frank," I said. "At least I know how bad it is. Is there anything I can do?"

"Pray?" he suggested quietly.

So pray I did. There was a large Catholic church in Woodford, on my route back to Epping. At least the rain had stopped and the draught of wind had dried me out pretty thoroughly. Inside the church the atmosphere was more gloomy – in terms of light and of the general chill and silence. I sat before the side altar, as I had been taught to by the nuns at school, and tried to pray for Piotr, and for my mother, and for my father and Henri, and for Anna, and for Anna's parents, and for Charlie. The list was long, and I'm not sure whether I was being heard. Finally I gave way to some real tears, and they ran freely and copiously, and I made no attempt to stop them. I sobbed. Probably loudly, because in a few minutes a priest appeared. He had a kindly look, red-faced and serious but not sombre. "Would you like to talk about it?" he asked softly. I nodded, though I did not know what to say. "Perhaps some tea would help," he suggested, and when I again nodded he took me through the sacristy and into what must have been a parlour or sitting room in the presbytery of the church. He asked me to sit while he went to fetch some tea, and when he returned I sipped it gratefully. "I don't think you live locally, do you?"

I told him a little about myself, and then tried to describe all that I had been praying about. As I said, it was a long list, but he listened patiently. Of course I did not tell him about what I believed about Anna's death, merely the fact of her fall in the farmyard at Houblions. But I did cover most of the rest of the names. He listened patiently, and asked one or two questions about things I did not explain clearly. I toyed in my mind with revealing the truth about Anna. I wanted someone to believe me, after all. But in the end I kept that part of my prayer a secret. He tried to comfort me, reminded me that everyone's journey through life is a pilgrimage, and sometimes a pilgrimage of sorrow. But the journey does continue, he said, and there had no doubt been joyous times on my journey, and he was sure there would be again. And for those others who are alive, even if very ill, he said, they too are on that pilgrims' route. We can help all those who are journeying alongside us, especially at such a time as this. It surprised me that his words did comfort me a little. They certainly steeled in me the determination to find and reveal Anna's killer. If I did that, perhaps I would help her parents. They must still be wondering how their daughter met such a cruel and untimely death.

I was thinking about Anna as I rode back to the farm, and I suddenly remembered that on that fateful last day she had said something to me during milking that was possibly significant. She'd asked to talk to me about something, but we had never held that conversation. I had jumped so quickly at the opportunity to go to North Weald to clear the damaged houses that I had forgotten about her request. I suppose I'd assumed it was more difficulty concerning her relationship with Charlie that had prompted her request to me. Now I would never know what she wanted to talk about. I hoped it wasn't something that might have prevented her death. That would be too much to bear.

I returned to the farm in time for the milking and ate my dinner in the kitchen in silence. I thought that any attempt to speak would lead me to say something about what I had discovered at the undertakers. I did not want to share that information over the dinner table. I knew the reaction it was likely to arouse.

CHAPTER 16
AUGUST 30TH 1940

The day of Anna's funeral was a strange, almost surreal, experience for all who attended the church. We had travelled together from the farm. Robert had driven his old Ford saloon out of the garage where it had been almost permanently since I arrived at the farm. It was so difficult to obtain fuel, he had explained once, that he'd all but given up on it. He and Susan sat in the front, and Charlie and I in the rear. Katherine had indicated that she did not wish to attend, and someone needed to be at the farm anyway. We travelled for most of the time in an uneasy silence. I guess we all knew what I thought about Anna's death and that made for an uneasy journey. They believed I held one of them responsible, but did not want to challenge me, and I still thought that they were the most obvious possible culprits, though I had no evidence to incriminate any of them, and I found it hard to believe that one of them had done so. Hence our unease with one another.

I was grateful to reach Romford, where Anna's parents lived and had raised her. The funeral service was to be held in the church of St Edward the Confessor in the centre of town, and I separated myself from the family and looked around the church, which was large and Gothic in style, with many carved heads of English kings and queens and other more esoteric figures. I gazed upwards towards the tower, which was high and steep, and I noted the stained glass windows, which had not been removed, though that might have been a wise move in our war-threatened time.

The church had started to fill, and there seemed to be many young women and a few men of around Anna's age, most of the men being in uniform. Anna's school friends, I guessed. Then above me a deep-sounding bell started to ring a solemn knell, and the undertaker and his men – all elderly and dressed in black – carried in Anna's coffin, followed by what must have been her family, her mother weeping and her father holding her arm firmly. Other relatives followed. The choir half-heartedly led the singing of "Abide with Me" and that set the tone for the service, but the difficulties really began as they finished their dirge. The now familiar high-pitched tone of an air-raid siren pierced the melancholy quiet of the church just as the priest was about to address the congregation. "Oh dear," he said, "I fear this means we have to evacuate to the shelter at the edge of the market place." We dutifully filed out but discovered that the one shelter that had been built

170

in the centre of town was already full before we reached it. We were left standing in the open for half an hour until an all-clear sounded, whereupon we all filed back into the church. Two minutes later the siren sounded again, and we left the church, but even as we walked towards the shelter the all-clear sounded again. "It's happening all the time like this," a woman walking next to me said. She looked at my Land Girl uniform. "I don't suppose you notice it out in the country." I told her that I was not working deep in the countryside, but I acknowledged that I was not subject to the tyrannies of the siren in the way we had been in the church that morning. When the sirens sounded for a third time, people were obviously reluctant to move, and the priest said that he would continue the service, though people were welcome to try to get into the shelter if they wanted.

I stayed, along with the majority of the congregation. But a few minutes later an ARP Warden came striding to the front of the church and beckoned the priest, who was in the middle of a homily about the fact that we all lived near to death, especially in times such as ours, and needed to acknowledge that in how we treated one another and lived our lives. I think he was just about to praise Anna for becoming a Land Girl and serving the country when the warden interrupted him. They spoke together in whispers for a couple of minutes, and then the Warden climbed up to the pulpit and told everyone that they had to leave. There was audible dissent from many in the congregation. We seemed to have entered some kind of standoff, with the Warden refusing to give way again to the priest and warning everyone that he had the law on his side, and the silent protest of the congregation and the priest, who had clearly had enough of the warnings and sirens.

Fortunately for us, the priest and the funeral service, the all-clear sounded. The Warden clearly heard it but did not want to give up his position of moral authority in the pulpit. Like others, I sensed, I was more doubtful about his legal authority. There had been many stories in the press of people ignoring the instructions of Wardens, often for good reasons, though sometimes just because of that anti-authoritarian sentiment that on occasion comes to the surface of the British mind. The priest called up to the Warden loudly enough for us all to hear, to remind him that the all-clear had sounded. The Warden reluctantly came down, but not before he had warned everyone present that they had broken the law, and that they needed to show more respect. "So should you," one of the young men in uniform shouted at him. "We're not here because we wanted to be. We're here because we have to be. It's a funeral!" His words won a ripple of applause, and cries of "Hear, hear," from those around him. The Warden stared angrily at him, but probably realised there was nothing to gain by staying, so turned sharply and stomped off. I suppose we were all left thinking on the general failure of the country to prepare adequately for war. The Norway campaign had been a disaster, the Expeditionary Force had suffered great losses and only been saved at the last minute by a fleet of volunteer rescue boats, and the fighter pilots were even then – as was evident from the sounding and resounding of sirens – fighting for their and our lives, when their own airfields had not been adequately prepared for defence, according to one of their own. The failure to build large enough air-raid shelters was just one more small sign of our often shambolic approach to the difficulties we faced.

The priest finished the service off, and the choir made a better effort at "Lord of All Hopefulness" than they had at the opening. The priest then announced the committal, which would take place at a cemetery nearby. I knew that Robert did not intend us to attend that, but rather to return to the farm. He was growing concerned about the harvest. He had already cut some of the hay, and we had forked it into rows, which were drying in its field, and we would need to stack it or bale the hay before the weather broke. I filed out with the rest of the congregation, following the coffin and the family. I thought of Anna's beauty – how transitory her glory had been. I had envied her attractiveness. And I could not help thinking again of that request she had made to me on her final day. I had dashed away and never responded. What had she wanted to say?

I passed with the others I was following in front of Anna's parents, who had stopped outside the church to thank people for attending the service. Her father shook my hand and muttered his thanks, but his wife stopped and asked me, "Are you Ginny, or Virginia, the other Land Girl?" When I nodded, she said "I'd like to thank you for being a good friend to Anna. I'm sorry it had to be you who discovered her." She had set crying aside, I could see, and was showing the resolution that we were all in need of.

"I'm glad if she saw me as a friend. We were thrown together by our work. Anna was changing, I think, as a result of being at the farm."

"I think you're right. She told us a lot, in her letters, you know."

I must have looked surprised. Anna's letters? I could not recall her writing letters. Her mother must have noticed my reaction, because she even half-smiled and said, "Anna was often writing. But you probably won't have noticed. She would not have wanted you to notice. She wrote either early in the morning or late at night when nobody would know."

"That's certainly true," I said. "I think it must have been in the mornings. She was always up before me." That was true. Indeed, sometimes she had to come back into our bedroom and shake me awake. Early morning was never my good time.

A sudden thought came to me. I couldn't bear to open the wounds of Anna's death there and then, outside the very church where we had tried to celebrate her short life. But it was possible that if Anna had written home she might have told her parents something that would shed light on her death. "I wonder," I said, "could I come and see you? At your home I mean, after today? We have to go back to the farm now. But I could probably cycle over here in a couple of days. I'd like to talk to you about Anna."

"That would be alright," she said. "We'd probably like to hear more about the last few weeks. And we have an air raid shelter in the garden, if these wretched sirens keep sounding." She reached into her bag and took out an old business card of her husband's. "It's got our address on," she explained as she passed it to me.

I moved on, for there were others who wanted to offer their condolences. I was looking for Robert and his family, to return to the car, but instead I was accosted by two middle-aged women. One was tall and thin, and dressed in mourning black from her lacy hat to her black leather shoes. The other was shorter and rounder, but likewise clothed in black. "Miss Beauchamp?" the taller woman asked me. When I confirmed that I was indeed the person they appeared to be seeking, they introduced themselves as being members of the Land Army Committee locally. They had come to pay their respects to a member of the Army who had suffered such a bad accident.

"Accident," I repeated, "How do you know it was an accident?"

My question startled them. They were momentarily unable to reply. They looked at me, and they looked about them as if a reply might appear on the face of one of the others from the congregation. Finally the taller one, who seemed the more dominant of the two, said, "Well of course it was an accident. The police and the coroner said so. You're not suggesting that…."

She trailed off and gestured towards Anna's parents. "Not here, in front of her parents." She approached me very closely and whispered the last words. "You're not suggesting that she killed herself!"

I stepped back in alarm. Why did everyone so misinterpret what I said? "No, of course I'm not," I protested. "I'm suggesting that there is more to her death than an accident, but not that she killed herself." I was whispering back at the pair of them, though hissing might better describe it. I was thoroughly fed up with being treated in this way, and my anger and guilt were getting the better of me. "I think someone killed her."

Now it was their turn to take a step back. They both looked at me, astonished but also somehow stony and cold. The tall thin one spoke again. "Don't be ridiculous, Miss Beauchamp. If the police thought someone had killed her, they'd have told us. We'd have been involved. Your safety would become an issue. But there has not been the remotest suggestion of murder." She tried to usher me away, not unreasonably, for there was a danger that we would be overheard, and I too did not want to create a scene. Neither Anna nor her parents would have deserved that at her funeral.

"Have it your way," I hissed again. "Believe those lazy policemen if you want. But I know that Anna would never have willingly gone near that drop from the barn. And...." I stopped myself in time. I did not want to share what I knew of the bruising on her face and arms.

"And...?" the shorter woman echoed me.

"Oh, and nothing. I can see that your minds are closed as well. But I will find out what happened. Anna deserves that." I turned away from them and sought out Robert, who was himself looking for me in the crowd. He obviously hoped to get some work done on the farm during the afternoon.

After another silent journey, we ate a quick lunch and Robert did indeed want us to start stacking the hay. He had picked a spot at the corner of the field and we had to toss the now dry hay into the trailer that he had attached to the tractor. Susan joined me and Katherine in gathering the hay with the lengthy forks that Robert provided, and Charlie drove the tractor while Robert commenced building the stack with the contents tipped from the trailer. The stack had to be built in a special way to prevent rain and moisture penetrating or staying within the stack. This hot and dusty work went on until milking, but once the last cow had returned to the fields Robert asked me to continue in the hay field while Susan prepared a late dinner, so that we worked away until half past eight in the evening. The sirens in Epping sounded twice, but we ignored them – funny how quickly one can abandon actions that just a few days previously would have appeared absolutely vital. And Hurricanes came and went from North Weald, no doubt refuelling before rejoining the battle that was being fought all that day with the Luftwaffe. The battles in the sky somehow made getting in the harvest even more vital, as it would be right across the kingdom. The hay would be needed for the cattle through the autumn and into the winter, to continue to produce milk, but Robert had already complained that he would probably have to cull the herd in March or April in order to plough up more fields for vegetables. Some of the hay fields would never produce hay again.

By the time we had finished, a good base to the stack had been established, and a fair portion of the field cleared down to stubble. It was too late to consider visiting the police. I kept my powder dry, therefore, and tried to make some conversation over dinner, however desultory. Charlie took himself off to the pub directly after eating. I wondered how early we would see him in the morning.

CHAPTER 17
AUGUST 31ST 1940

Next morning Robert said that Will, the lorry driver who carted the milk churns, was making a delivery that afternoon to Royal Wanstead School, an orphanage that was near Whipps Cross Hospital. He had asked him to take me there, knowing that I was visiting a patient there, and if I kept my visit short, Will might even pick me up and bring me back in time for milking and more stacking if it was needed. I thanked him and, the weather being fine and there having been no dewfall, we resumed the hay-stacking once the milking had been done and breakfast was over, all four of us again working in our respective roles. Charlie was particularly truculent, probably because of the late-night drinking session he had indulged in. Robert asked Katherine to drive the tractor and Charlie took himself off for a walk, or a drink, or both perhaps.

As Susan and I worked together, she told me that Charlie had again threatened to join up. He was fed up being the object of scorn from the older men in the pub who had fought in the Great War. If he left, though, they would struggle to maintain the farm because Charlie now did so much of the heaviest work. Robert would find it hard to manage the changes that WarAg were demanding and the maintenance work. She hoped that, despite all that had happened, I would stay on and they would then be able to ask for more members of the Land Army. That was their only hope of getting enough labour to keep going. Otherwise Robert was thinking of leasing some of the land out to one or more other farmers, or he would refuse WarAg's instructions and go to their MP for support, especially if Charlie did enlist.

I was sympathetic to their dilemma. I'm sure that similar problems were occurring for families up and down the country. Managing a war of the scale and intensity that the country was facing meant enormous disruption. But when you are directly involved in one family's problems, the matter becomes much more personal, and you can see how their relationships and the changes the war was forcing on them were affecting them adversely. Robert and Susan and Charlie were facing a period of turmoil and uncertainty and might be dependent on the goodwill of the Land Army. And I could not see what lay in the future for them or for me, because I could not convince anybody of what had happened to Anna. And until I resolved that, I did not think that I could determine anything else.

Robert said that in the afternoon he would cut the hay in the next field, which eventually he wanted to bale and bring into the barn. Then on Sunday, if I would give them the morning, we could all lay the cut hay into the strands in which it would dry. Next week it should be fit for baling, if the good weather held. So I was free to go with Will, and Susan provided a sandwich and a small cake that she had baked earlier in the week. At the last minute she gave me another of the cakes. "For your airman," she said, "If he can eat." I thanked her and went out of the farm to Will's. I knocked on his door and after a minute or so I knocked again. A muffled shout came from within, but since the door was locked I was forced to wait until he came out. He had obviously been dozing, and was a little dishevelled, still buttoning his shirt and tying his shoelaces. He half-smiled at me and then told me to get in the cab of the lorry and wait for him there.

It was a full ten minutes before he appeared again, drawing on a cigarette which he threw at the roadside, before mounting to the cab and sitting alongside me. "You're for the hospital, then?" he checked with me as he turned the ignition. "I'm going close by as Robert must have told you." We then proceeded in silence along the old coaching road from Newmarket to London, passing various public houses at crossroad points. At each one Will muttered a short description of the pub and its landlord. Some he obviously favoured; others he most definitely did not. Otherwise there was no conversation until we had passed Woodford and were, he assured me, almost there.

Without taking his eyes off me he suddenly said, "Robert's been talking to me. About that other girl's death. He says you don't think it was an accident, and that you've been telling the police she was murdered."

"That's not quite the case," I protested, once my surprise at the sudden challenge had died down. "I've just said that there are some odd aspects to Anna's death that cause me concern."

"That's as may be," he said, emphasising both the last words separately, "but I urge you to drop it now. They've enough to worry about without you causing more trouble. The police said it was an accident. You could leave the matter alone now. Robert and Susan are worried about the future of the farm, and your raising questions is making their worry worse."

Well I knew all that, and I hadn't really needed him to remind me. It was one of the things that was worrying me. But I still felt my greater loyalty was with the dead Anna. And I had not expected Will, who was really a complete stranger to me, suddenly to try to direct me as he had.

"I'm a friend of theirs," he said. "That's why I'm raising it with you. They need you to ."

"Anything I agree to do I'll agree with them and not with you, however friendly you are. If there's something wrong with Anna's death, someone needs to find out."

He became more animated when I said that. "You'll lose them their business and like as not me my home if you keep meddling. In case you didn't know I rent my home from them. If the farm is sold, I lose my home. So that's another reason why I'm asking you to stop interfering." He sounded anxious and upset, so I remained silent. He obviously felt that he had said what was necessary, and said nothing more until he dropped me at the roadside where he was about to turn left, telling me to be at the same spot in an hour's time. I recognised that I was just three hundred yards from the hospital, and walked along by the forest side to reach the entrance.

To my relief Piotr was a little better, or at least that's what the nurse told me. His face was a little thinner, I thought, and he looked pale rather than feverish. I suppose that was an improvement. He was still very weak, and he did not much raise his head from the pillow while I was at his side. He was able to acknowledge me, though, and he did ask me about any news from the war, and especially from North Weald. I told him that I had not heard anything from North Weald, because Roger had not been in touch. I also told him that the Hurricanes were still flying and fighting regularly, often several times a day, and I told him about Anna's funeral in Romford. He laughed quietly when I told him of the inadequacy of the air-raid shelter, and muttered something about the British not being any better prepared than the Poles had been, and when would they learn, but I tried not to be drawn into that discussion. Instead I told him about the bruising I had seen on Anna's face and arm, and my anger that no-one would listen to me and do anything. It was the only moment that he became roused, and he half-sat up. "Be careful, Ginny," he warned, "if someone did her harm they might do it to you as well. Be careful." Then he sank back on the pillow. I tried to reassure him, though I was not much reassured myself. Piotr's warnings had a tendency to come true in the end. Look at what he'd said about the defence of the airfield. I thought it best to change the subject and talked about the harvesting of the hay. He listened and showed some interest, though that started to wane as I wittered on rather. I guessed he was tiring, and my time was almost up. I therefore drew my tale to a close and started to make my farewell. He revived momentarily and asked for a kiss. I pecked him politely on the cheek. "No, no, he insisted, "a proper kiss." So I kissed him on the lips, and this time when his tongue sought out mine, I reciprocated. He must be recovering, I concluded.

Will was quite a few minutes late in picking me up, and I was wondering if he had decided to reinforce his words by abandoning me there. It would have taken me quite a while to get back to Epping, and the second half of my mission for that afternoon would have foundered. He did turn up, eventually, and explained that the cook at the orphanage had offered him a meal through gratitude at his delivery of the food. I wondered if he sought out such gratuities wherever he delivered but did not comment on it. Instead I stayed silent, as did he, until we neared Epping. I asked him to drop me near the High Street because I had some purchases I had to make. "Just remember what I said," he said as I alighted. "Please stop interfering in matters and get on with your work. That's what we all need." His tone was pleading, but insistent.

Unfortunately for him his words were the proverbial water off a duck's back: I was headed straight for the police station, not for the shops. Once again I had to wait for someone to come and see me, and this time it was a rather old and portly sergeant, not one of the officers I had seen before. I had great difficulty explaining the whole situation – he did not appear ever to have heard of Anna's death, let alone of my previous concerns. Having finally persuaded him that there was a possible issue if her body was carrying bruises in the shape of fingers, he shuffled off to consult someone. I suspected it was one of the officers I had seen, but who was refusing to come out and talk to me. Within a few minutes he came back to me and said that he'd been told that I had already aired my concerns and that they would not be listened to any further. I must stop bothering them. They had enough work to do with the bombing at North Weald, and I should stop wasting their time. That was that, was the look he had on his face. And when I left the station I could have sworn that the face of one of the officers I had previously talked to watched me from an upstairs window, as if making sure that I had left.

I was smarting as I left. I felt that during the months since I joined the Land Army I had suffered one rebuff after another. The ones that affected me personally were annoying. The ones concerning Anna's death were alarming. No-one seemed concerned that a young woman, fit and in full command of her senses, had died in such strange circumstances. Well, no-one but me! And the authorities whom I tried to provoke into action simply regarded me as a combination of pathetic female and troublesome woman. I thought I had just two more shots to fire, and in the next two days I would fire them both: Anna's parents and Scotland Yard.

CHAPTER 18
SEPTEMBER 1ST 1940

The Land Army had obviously still made no decision about replacing Anna, and strictly speaking I was due to have part of Sunday off. It was Katherine's day off and she was visiting her family. I negotiated with Robert that I would share the milking with him and that I would work on the harvest with him, Charlie and Susan until one o'clock. Then I was spared the remainder of the day. I looked up the address that Anna's mother had given me in a street map that stood on the dresser in the kitchen and tried to memorise the final part of the route. I changed into some civilian clothing to cycle to Romford, and knowing the route between Epping and Romford better after my previous visits, I set off. As I left the farm I heard the air-raid siren sounding, but I rode on, listening for the sound of any bomber overhead. There was little traffic on the road. The fuel shortage had stopped almost all social driving. Cars for the most part were only used for vital or professional purposes, and there were very few vans or lorries moving about on a Sunday. I was passed by a lorry-load of troops who called out to me – not every shout was complimentary or even savoury – and one or two cars carrying what looked from the hats and suits and ties, like churchgoers returning home from a service. Otherwise I had a pleasant ride, and at times almost forgot my purpose. As I neared Romford a formation of British fighters flew southwards overhead. They were Hurricanes I think, or at least they looked like the aircraft that I had seen flying out of North Weald so often. Pleasant Sunday or not, the war was continuing around me.

Anna's parents welcomed me a little formally, but then they had just lost the treasure of their lives and I was an obvious reminder of the fact. I had determined that while I would seek any information that might help me, I would make it my main aim to tell them more about Anna's work, her relationship with Charlie and the obvious happiness she showed at times, and her consistent beauty. I therefore tried to introduce all these ideas when her mother had made us tea and poured it out in the front living room that was obviously only used when there were guests in the house. I described how we did the milking each day, and how we carried the churns to and fro, and then the general work of hoeing, ditching, spraying, tending, cutting and so on with which our days had been filled. I passed over the early days of my time at the farm, when Anna would go AWOL at times, but I did tell them that Anna was not happy at first because of the conflict with Charlie's parents. They surprised me with their knowledge of all this, however, and told me that Anna had told them about it. She had also praised me, and said that I was a valued friend, which made me feel rather guilty.

At this point in our conversation the local sirens started their piercing wailing. "Oh dear," Anna's mother said, "that means we should move to the shelter." They stood up and I followed their lead, but not into the street (I had anticipated that there was a communal shelter somewhere nearby). Rather they lead me into the back garden where a mound of piled earth showed me where they had installed an Anderson shelter. There were steps leading down to the entrance, with planks allowing a steady footing as we descended. The corrugated iron was visible, but the roof was indeed piled high with earth – I assumed it was the earth displaced in digging out the space for the shelter – and they had planted vegetables in the earth, so that a small crop of food could be harvested. I noted that most of the garden had been converted into a vegetable patch. Inside the shelter they had some kind of oil lamp, which they lit, and some old chairs sitting on the duckboards on the floor. "It's very wet underneath," Anna's mother said. We're not sure it will be useable in the winter, but for the moment we can."

We sat in the shelter and looked at one another. I decided that I needed to move the conversation on to the matter of Anna's death, however uncomfortable our circumstances were for such a painful discussion. "I think what I'm about to say may upset you. I'm sorry if that is the case, but it is really necessary that I say it. One of the reasons I came today," I said nervously, "is that, despite the fact that it was I who discovered Anna that night, I'm not sure that her death was purely accidental." In the gloom I sensed that they both stiffened, but they said nothing. "Anna suffered from vertigo. She told me that when we were set to work in the hayloft. She would not go near the gap in the wall that was used for winching. I don't believe that she would have gone anywhere near it in the night." I stopped talking to try to gauge their reaction. For a few moments they too were silent.

It was Anna's father who spoke first. "Yes she did, but the police said that she might have been waiting to meet the farmer's son, Charlie. She had met him up in the hayloft before." There was a pause. "We understand that she and Charlie were courting. We know what courting couples are like. It would be no surprise if they went up there to meet and …." His voice trailed away. I nodded, though I'm not sure he could see me. There were probably some tears falling, so it was perhaps just as well that it was semi-dark in the shelter.

"I know, I know," I muttered, "I'm not surprised if they met there, but they would have been at the back of the barn, not near the winch. Anna was clearly terrified of that area. Did the police say that she was meeting Charlie there?"

"No. They said that he had categorically denied it."

"I hope that everyone involved in this is telling the truth," I said, deliberately ambivalent in my judgement of Charlie's assertion. "But I just can't see why she would go anywhere near the winch even if they did have an assignation. It just makes no sense. I've tried raising it with the police, but they interpret me all wrong, and then tell me to drop it. But there is something more." Now I was going to enter a very sensitive area. "I went to see Anna, in the funeral directors. I saw marks on her face," I hesitated because Anna's mother had gasped. "And on her arm. They did not look to me like any marks that could have been caused by her fall."

There was silence. A long silence. Anna's mother was wiping her eyes with a handkerchief. I apologised if I had upset them and feared that they might become angry with me. But Anna's mother protested, "No, you haven't. It's just that we couldn't bring ourselves to visit her. She was so beautiful, we did not want to see her in that way. So we didn't notice anything. What you've said has come as a shock, but not altogether a surprise. We'd accepted what the police said, but when we talked about it, then yes her fear of heights, and especially of looking out and down from a height, was something we wondered about. But we accepted the story about her waiting to meet her boyfriend."

There was another long silence, broken – fortunately – by the all-clear. Anna's father supported her mother in climbing up the steps, and we resumed our seats in the front room. He was obviously trying to think things through. "You said you'd raised concerns, Virginia, but got nowhere. Is that right?"

"Yes. I told the police and I told the Land Army. I also told the family. I'm not very popular as a result."

"We can only thank you for doing so. I am worried for you though. If someone did Anna harm, might they not want to do you harm as well if you are crying wolf, as you have done? Aren't you placing yourself at risk? We can't do anything to bring Anna back, but you can save yourself from harm."

"But it doesn't seem right. It just does not sit well with me to drop it."

"What if we asked you to? For your own safety? We know from Anna's letters how much she liked you. We do not want anything bad to happen to you as well."

"I'm going to make one more attempt to raise my concerns about it all. If that fails, I suppose I may have to give up. I don't want to, but I haven't got any evidence that points to a likely culprit. In those early weeks after my arrival you'll be aware that there was conflict, and you could have identified some possible suspects, but not in recent weeks. Everything had settled down."

Anna's father left the room for a while, and her mother came over and sat next to me on the sofa where I had been sitting on my own. "I do understand what Anna was doing. I'm her mother. I think she had made a big decision about herself and Charlie. I could read between the lines, but my husband couldn't. I haven't told him what I guessed at. I listened to you very carefully. You know all about it, I think, but I respect you all the more for the polite way in which you've said everything. I'm not upset by it. Women have to make such decisions at certain times. Anna was clearly happy with Charlie. She thought she had found herself. So all this has been very upsetting." She stopped and looked at me. "Don't put yourself at risk as well. Do what the police have said and drop it." Then she hugged me, hard and long. When she let me go she gave a little shake of her head, as if to remind me to stop. It seemed like a good moment to leave, and I stood up and brushed myself down to prepare myself. She led me into the hallway and her husband appeared again. He urged me once more to leave the matter alone, and I agreed to do so if my final card failed to win a trick. Of course, I had not mentioned that Anna's and Charlie's affair had not really been consummated, or at least not happily so. I'd caused enough pain already.

With a very heavy heart, I recall, I cycled back to Epping. Anna's parents had accepted her death. They were not totally surprised by my anxieties about the matter, but they had been directed somewhat in their thoughts by the police. Their concern for me was touching. I was not sure I deserved it. I had not always supported Anna, perhaps especially when she might have needed my assistance. I had been resentful at times. I had not responded to her final request to me, to speak to her that day. Perhaps if I had, whatever befell her would not have occurred. I reached the farm as darkness was falling, and I took my black thoughts with me to my bedroom.

CHAPTER 19
SEPTEMBER 2ND 1940

I did not think that I would be able to negotiate with Robert an absence that would allow me to visit Scotland Yard. He told me while we were milking the cattle that he wanted to finish as much of the harvesting as possible. Forecasts had suggested that the weather would break soon, and he wanted to use all five of us to complete the baling of the hay. I had therefore to mull over my situation during the morning while Susan, Katherine and I forked the dry hay into piles and then into the trailer, the repetitive action tiring but no longer hurting my arms and back. I was not due any more time off for a fortnight; I needed to visit Scotland Yard because I thought that if I spoke to a detective there, he might be more prepared to look into the matter than the Epping police and coroner had been; I could only make such a visit during working hours; I would therefore have to create a pretext for leaving, and I might as well do it that day as wait any longer. I thought I owed it to Anna's parents either to obtain some response from the most famous detectives in the land, or give up as they had urged me to. When we broke for some lunch, I asked if I could use the telephone to phone the hospital and check on Piotr. I said that I had been concerned by his condition on the Saturday. I knew that Robert, Susan and Charlie would not be returning to the farmhouse: they would be eating sandwiches in the field where we were working.

I went in and out of the farmhouse just in case one of them had followed me back, but I did not phone the hospital. I waited a minute or two and then went and changed, left a note explaining that I had gone to the hospital because Piotr was even worse, grabbed my cycle and hurried to the station where I caught the first of the connecting trains I needed into London. The journey took a while. The train went slowly and there were several long delays when the train stood idle somewhere between stations. The driver sent messages via the guard that we were being held up by air-raid warnings ahead of us. The whole life of the country was being badly affected by the threat of the Luftwaffe. It was mid-afternoon before I reached Scotland Yard, and I hesitated outside, attempting through the quick application of some make-up to make myself look more adult and serious. I knew that I had become quite tanned during the summer, and anyone not knowing that I was a Land Girl might think I had been lazing around in a deckchair somewhere. I needed even a reception clerk to take me seriously.

There was a large reception desk just beyond the entrance. It did not have a clerk but a desk sergeant in full uniform. He had a very military bearing, and a stern face, but he was attentive to me when I approached. A tall man in a dark double-breasted suit had been talking to him, and he too turned towards me. Perhaps the make-up was working, I thought. "How can I help you?" the sergeant asked. Stupid me! Even on the journey into London, I could have thought about what exactly I needed to say. But I hadn't. I'd sat on the train empty-headed, thoughtless, witless!

"I suppose I've come to report a crime," I managed to blurt out. "A serious crime. A possible murder." The sergeant looked sceptical. But the other man was looking at me with interest. "Yes, really, something happened to a young woman I was working with, as a Land Girl, and I think it may not have been an accident." I looked earnestly at the sergeant, while the man with him stared at me, his eyes squinting.

The sergeant was obviously weighing up what I had said. I hoped I didn't look like some lunatic, a fantasist or a trouble-maker. Perhaps he was thinking about the same thing. "All right," he said finally, "I'll see if someone will see you. Take a chair over there, would you? What's your name, by the way?"

"Beauchamp, Virginia Beauchamp."

The sergeant waved me over to some chairs, and I went to sit down. The man in the suit followed me. I could see that the suit was a little shabby, but his shoes were polished and his hair neatly combed. "Always check a man's shoes, Ginny," my father would say to me. "You can tell a lot about a man from his shoes."

The man sat near to me and looked at me again. "You must be, you have the look of him, the daughter of Captain Beauchamp, the officer in the Royal Leicestershire, the Tigers?"

I was stunned. I'd been told that I looked like a mixture of my mother and my father, but I had never been recognised in this way. This man must have known my father some twenty-odd years previous to our meeting. I suppose my father was younger then. It did not appeal to me that I might look like the late middle-aged version of the Beauchamp family that he now represented. But the younger, more dashing and handsome infantry captain, well that wasn't so bad. I agreed that I was indeed his daughter, and the man held his hand out to me. "Detective Superintendent Williamson," he said by way of introduction. "I was a sergeant in your father's company. He...he..." the man hesitated, while I urged him on with my gestures, "he saved my life, saved it twice actually. What a remarkable coincidence to bump into you here and now. Is he well?"

"He is and doing some important work for the Air Ministry. He doesn't tell me anything about it." That was a slight lie, but since I hardly saw my father those days it seemed like a complete truth. "But tell me, how did he save your life?"

"Once, when a gas canister exploded near us. I was fumbling with my mask and failing to fit it properly. Got some in the lungs and the eyes, in fact. He grabbed me, took the mask in his hands, and fitted it properly. I would not have survived that mustard gas. Horrible stuff!" He shuddered as if remembering the moment.

"And the other occasion?"

"Well, I will tell you Miss Beauchamp, though you might spare me his wrath if you don't tell him it was I who told you this. He saved me and the whole squad we were with by deliberately not hearing a command." He looked at me as if he were concerned about what he had just said. "I hope that doesn't trouble you. It was the right thing to do. The command was an insane one, to attack a whole nest of machine-guns entrenched on a ridge, when we had no grenades and were desperately short of ammunition. A messenger had been sent up to us, who were an advance squad trying to clear the way for the rest of the company. But the machine guns had already wiped out the whole of the first squad to attack them. We would have gone the same way if we'd obeyed that order. Only he and I and another sergeant had heard the order before the messenger went back. "He did say we were not to attack, didn't he?" your father said to us. I'll never forget his look. It bore right into me. "Yes," I said, "we were not to attack." And the other sergeant agreed. So we left two men to wait for the rest of the company and took a skirting route around the machine guns. The two left behind told the company about this, but the CO still insisted on sending men to attack the machine guns. Lost twenty men before he gave up and followed us. He gave your father a very hard time over it, but he stuck to his guns and I and the other sergeant backed him up. Any attack would just have been organised suicide. A good man, your father. He wouldn't have disobeyed orders normally, but there and then he made a decision that saved my life. I'm very pleased to meet you. Perhaps you'll remember me to your father. Give him this if you would, please." He took out a cardboard business card, which had his name, title and position, and the address and telephone number.

"I don't suppose you can help me with my problem?" I asked.

"About a suspicious death? No, I can't really. I'm not with the murder squad. But if you need some particular help, use the card. Call me and I'll see what I can do. My driver is just turning up at the door, so I must go. I can't see well enough to drive, because of that gas in the first war. So I'm reliant on finding a spare driver. They'd have pensioned me off, I'm sure, if it weren't for this war. Goodbye, and good luck with the problem you're raising."

He had lifted my spirits a little, but I'm sorry to say that everything went downhill after he departed. I was called to an interview room by a red-faced, sweaty detective constable, whose breath smelled of beer and cigarettes, and who listened to my story with a scornful look on his face. When I said that the police in Epping and the coroner had decided it was an accident, he interrupted me and asked why I was there at all. If they had called it an accident, it was an accident. Who was I to countermand them? If I was a Land Girl, why wasn't I on my farm working instead of wasting everyone's time? He showed me out within ten minutes, I would guess. If anything, he was worse than the Epping police. At least they had heard me out before dismissing me.

I returned to Epping very sad, and very angry. I had so wanted to obtain some form of justice for Anna and for her parents. Her death seemed a tragedy in the midst of a wider tragedy, the war, and just as I had been denied any right to participate directly in the war effort, so she had been denied her right to live. I did not suppose that it would be the last death I would see – I knew what had gone on in Poland, remember – but my inability to obtain any official recognition of her death as suspicious was frustrating. No, it was maddening.

On my return I was faced by a furious Robert. He did not think I'd done right by just leaving a note and rushing off to the hospital. I should have spoken with him about it before doing so. They had not managed to finish the harvest, and he was upset about that. If the weather broke, the hay left in the field would never recover fully, even if we managed to dry it. He had called the Land Army to say that he would not pay my full wages for that week. I pointed out, not unreasonably I thought, that I had worked more than my set hours on several occasions, that I was having to do more to make up for the absence of another Land Girl. Far from stopping my wages, I told him that he should be paying me extra for the work I had been doing. I said I was angry!

Robert did not like my argument. Perhaps it was too close to the truth, and that made him uncomfortable, but he retorted that he had already called the Land Army people, and that he would not pay me any extra. I had let myself and them down, in his view. My heart sank when he said that. I'd had one warning. My Land Girl position must now be in jeopardy, I realised.

CHAPTER 20
SEPTEMBER 3RD & 4TH
1940

Next morning it was raining, a slow drizzle that looked as if it might last for some time. Robert felt that his fears for the remainder of the harvest had come true and he let me know of his unhappiness in no uncertain terms as we brought the cattle in. I decided to say nothing in response. I suspected my comeuppance was really yet to arrive. When we had finished the milking in sullen silence and transported the churns down to the collection point, I went into the kitchen for a miserable breakfast. I felt stupid and naïve that I had so pressed people about Anna that I had done myself harm, and I was angry with myself and with the world for not solving the riddle of her death. Susan and Katherine said nothing to me, and Robert and Charlie stayed away. It was as if we were all waiting for the consequences of Robert's call to the Land Army to unravel. And it did not take long.

I had gone down to the fields to do some hedging work, because in the late summer sun the borders of the fields had been growing extensively. I had been there about an hour when I heard Robert in the distance calling me, and when I looked, he waved me back to the farmhouse. It was a walk of shame I had done before of course – twice in schools, and once in the Magistrate's Court. I don't recommend it. You feel as if your stomach is down in your feet, and yet you might be sick any moment. You know what's coming but you don't want to hear it. You don't want to be a participant in the ritual of humiliation and blame, but you know you have to be there. You are the necessary victim and anti-hero of this particular theatrical event.

In the farmyard there were a man and a woman waiting for me. The man was from the WarAg committee I think, though he did not introduce himself. I guess he had done the driving and was going to talk to Robert about what was to happen next. The woman told me that she was Mrs Emily Wright, and she had been sent by Lady Wakeham. Complaints about me had been received from two other members of the committee who said I had been provocative and pestered them at Anna's funeral; from the Epping police that I had been fruitlessly pressing a ridiculous claim that Anna had been killed, not died in an accident; from a Scotland Yard detective for the same reason; and from the farmer Robert Williams that I had gone AWOL. She had decided, because I had received a warning previously, that I should be dismissed immediately from the Women's Land Army. I was to leave the farm as soon as I had packed, and she would supervise my departure. I would have to return my uniform and Army paraphernalia to the centre where I had originally signed up. She gave me a document that stated all this formally and gave me my instructions. She was also going to remove Anna's belongings and return them to her parents. She did at least offer me a lift to the station, realising that I would struggle to carry my things there.

Robert, Susan and Charlie had gathered by the kitchen door to listen to all this. Katherine was standing by the door to her room. Robert was looking stony-faced, Susan embarrassed, and Charlie rather anguished. I had had enough though. I turned to all of them, and shouted, "I don't care what you all say, think or do. A young woman was killed here. She did not die in an accident. She had vertigo – she would not have dared to approach that opening." I pointed at the winch above us all. "And I saw the marks on her face and arm. They were not bruises caused by a fall. They matched someone's fingers, someone's hands: the someone who killed her."

I turned and marched off to start to pack my things. They all stood silent and watching me, all except Charlie who followed me and overtook me, stopping me as I approached my quarters. "Say that again," he demanded, though not menacingly. "About her face and arm, say it again."

"She had bruises on her face that matched the fingers of a hand, and I don't think they were caused by her fall. And similar marks on her arm."

"I saw the bruises on her face," he said, half to himself. "I didn't think about them. I didn't think at all." He turned back, and I watched him. He walked past his parents and the two visitors and turned down towards the road. Only when he was out of sight did I enter my quarters and start to pack my suitcase.

I was interrupted by Mrs Wright, who had brought a spare case for Anna's things. I showed her where Anna had stored her case and her clothes, and I completed my packing and lugged the heavy case out of the bedroom, through the door into the yard and across to the kitchen door. The yard was empty now, and I sat on my case, feeling truly miserable. I had really messed up this time. What would my father say? What would Henri say? And Piotr? And Roger? And Lewi? In some way I thought I had let them all down.

It took Mrs Wright quite a time to pack Anna's things and get them and my case into the car. Then she ushered me into the back seat and went to fetch the man from WarAg to drive us away. He still said nothing to me, though he shook Robert's hand. Robert went back into the house and I was left to an unmarked, unwatched exit from the farm. I did not shed any tears. I was still too angry to cry. I fumed the whole drive to the station, clambered out, picked my case out of the boot and left the two from WarAg and Land Army without a backward glance. My anger did not melt during my journey either. Once again air-raid warnings punctuated the route into town, and the changeovers were delayed by twenty minutes both times. I felt exhausted by the time I reached my father's apartment, and on balance I was grateful that neither he nor Henri were there. They had left a note saying that they would not be back until the weekend. Only when I thought of Henri did I realise that I had left my cycle at the farm. I would have to return next day to collect it and bring it back to Victoria. I did find some food in the refrigerator, and I cooked myself some eggs and potatoes. I had no desire for food but knew that I would grow weak if I did not eat something. In normal times I would have cheered myself by having a bath, or calling a London friend and inviting them over, but I could not do either. I went to bed and cried myself to sleep.

Next morning I was sluggish as if I'd had a heavy night with a group of friends. I hadn't. And I had only rarely felt less sociable in my life. The combination of sorrow, guilt, anger and humiliation is not a good one, let me tell you. All those emotions were raging within me, and probably some others that I can't even remember. I dragged some clothes on and did some make-up in a desultory manner. Not even that could make me feel any better. I drank some tea, made some porridge but then couldn't face it, and instead dunked some dry biscuits I found in a tin in a second cup of tea. I had resolved to try to walk to Liverpool Street, using the bank of the Thames as my guide, just because the train was so slow and the stops within the tunnels were so hot and airless. It proved a good idea at first, and as I walked between Parliament Square and the river I remembered Wordsworth's poem about crossing the Bridge, and how the sight of London had lifted his spirits. If I had been feeling cheerful I think I could have completed that part of my journey on foot, but as I reached the area just south of St Paul's I was very tired. I waited for a while, and then took a train for the last couple of stops before changing to the line going east, first to Leytonstone, and then to Epping. I immediately headed for the farm, though I felt distinctly nervous about my likely reception there.

It was just my luck that Robert and Charlie were working on the tractor in the yard as I walked around the corner. Robert saw me immediately and challenged me. "What are you doing back here?" he bellowed. "You've been chucked out. Get out of here!"

"I've only come for my cycle," I said meekly, trying not to inflame his anger. "I left it here yesterday."

"Get it and go, then," he shouted again. Susan appeared at the door, obviously having heard his shouting. "It's because of you that we're in such difficulty." He was still shouting. I did not know the detail, but I guessed his discussion with WarAg and the Land Army the day before had not gone well. Perhaps he was not going to get the additional labour he needed.

I held my arms out in a kind of plea. "No it is not my fault," I said firmly. "Whatever has happened is a reflection of the conflict and arguments that used to go on here, and the fact that a Land Girl has died here. I was just trying to unravel the mystery. But no-one would listen to me. That's not my fault."

Robert looked about to reply but to my surprise Charlie intervened. "Leave it. Dad, she may have a point. I told you yesterday that I think she may have a point about the bruising on Anna. So leave it! She's suffered enough, as have we." This last point was aimed at me. I nodded. I probably had contributed to the troubles that had beset us all. Charlie added, "They won't give us any Land Girls for two months. But WarAg are still saying we've got to plough up five more fields for vegetables to be planted for next year. That's why he's upset. That, and everything else."

"I'm sorry. I'm very sorry. If I have caused any of this I do apologise, but you know that I was only concerned to find out what had happened to Anna, and I was pretty useless at doing that."

"He knows that really." Charlie was speaking as if his father wasn't there. "In fact part of his frustration is that they sacked you, and he had reported you. You were a good farm worker. You did everything you were asked to and some more. I just wish it hadn't happened."

I went into the barn and retrieved my cycle. When I came out with it Susan had approached closer. She held out my ration cards. "I got them back for you. I was going to post them on to you. But you can take them now. You'll need them wherever you go."

There was nothing more to say. I mounted the cycle and left them. My bottom lip was probably trembling. I was grateful, though, for what Charlie had said. I hadn't thought that he had it in him to speak up like that. Other than Anna's parents, no-one had given my concern the time of day. Perhaps Charlie would find out more in time. Who knows, he might discover the culprit, I hoped.

I was at least able to visit Piotr. I cycled to Whipps Cross, and locked the cycle to a fence. In the ward Piotr was asleep, and he stayed asleep for the whole hour I was there. "You shouldn't worry about him sleeping now," the nurse said to me. "It's quite a good sign now he's recovering. I always think of it as the patient recharging their batteries. He's rebuilding his strength." It still meant that I couldn't talk to him. Couldn't kiss him either. But I would not have known what to tell him of my own situation. I still had a sick feeling inside as I headed off for the station and the journey home.

With the cycle I could ride home from Liverpool Street, and I stopped and bought some meat and vegetables on the way. I would at least eat properly that night. Next day I purposed to visit Anna's parents again, and to tell them of my dismissal and my decision to give the matter up. I could not see how I could continue to pursue it.

It was around half-past seven and I was slowly stewing the food in some red wine that I had filched from my father's supply, when the doorknocker sounded. I was surprised, but opened the door, ready to push it back if it was somebody I didn't like the look of. But It was Lewi! Yes, Lewi. "What are you doing here?" I said without thinking.

"Well, that's a fine welcome," she smiled as she said it. "Couldn't you do a better greeting than that?"

I apologised. I apologised twice. "Oh God," I said, "you must have heard!"

She nodded. "Yes, that you'd got yourself into trouble again. Miss Capthorn couldn't resist telling me. I guessed, and I hoped, that you'd be here." With that she hugged me tightly, and I think kissed my cheek. I pulled her into the living room and we sat down on the sofa. "Tell me about it, if you feel able to." And for an hour, with some breaks to check the meat, I told her Anna's story, and my story, and Charlie's story, so that she understood. When I had finished she asked me, "What next? What are you going to do?"

"I'm going to visit Anna's parents tomorrow to tell them that I can't do any more, and then I'll talk it all over with my father at the weekend and see if he has any suggestions. I'm not looking forward to telling him, though. It will confirm some of his fears about me being reckless and thoughtless."

"I'll get a petition up, among the Girls, all those I can find. It's not right that they've dismissed you. You were just trying to find out the truth about another Land Girl and her death. We can all understand that."

"No, Lewi, you'll just get yourself into trouble. But I am grateful for the thought. I must work this out on my own. Now, are you ready to eat?"

I served the food, and we polished off the bottle of my father's claret. And another bottle. Before we thought, or at least I thought, about how Lewi was getting home.

"I'm not," she said with certainty. "I decided I was staying the moment you opened the door. Is there a spare bed?"

"Not really," I answered. "I can't put you in my father's room, or Henri's."

"What about yours? Haven't you got a big enough bed?"

I had, of course, because I liked a large bed even though I never shared it with anyone. But Lewi was insistent, and we were both a little tipsy, so we stacked the plates and dishes and went to bed. I think in our drunkenness, and our innocence, we both took a little pleasure in stripping off our clothes and changing into pyjamas, showing off the muscles we had developed during our work. And we fell into bed together, holding each other, and fell asleep. I had the best night's sleep for quite some time. I can't speak for Lewi. I hope she did too.

CHAPTER 21
SEPTEMBER 5ᵀᴴ-6ᵀᴴ 1940

Lewi told me in the morning that she had informed Miss Capthorn that there was a bit of a family crisis at home, and that she should not expect her back until the afternoon, so we took a little time over breakfast, and enjoyed each other's company. I was able to tell her how grateful I was for her visit, and how it had cheered me up, and she said she was glad to do so. As soon as she had heard the outline of what had happened to me, she knew she had to track me down. When we were ready I accompanied her to Victoria station, and we started our laborious journeys together. On the train Lewi said to me that her favourite Shakespearean heroine was Viola, who at the start of the play "Twelfth Night" is shipwrecked, washed up on a foreign shore, bereft of family, possessions, well…everything. But she is spirited, energetic and sympathetic, and she triumphs through the comic events of the play. "As you left Raines Hall on that

Sunday," Lewi said, "I thought of Viola. I'm sure you can get through all that has been thrown at you. You are Viola, for me at least." I think I still had tears of gratitude in my eyes as we separated at Liverpool Street. Once more I had taken my cycle, thinking that I might again visit Piotr.

I found Anna's house and to my relief her mother answered the door. "Virginia, we weren't expecting you. James isn't here. He's gone into work, for the first time since...."

"I should have called you, I think," I answered, "but it doesn't matter if he isn't here. Can I come in?"

"Of course, of course." She brought me into the kitchen this time. Women's intimacy, I think. No need for the formality of the front room, but she would not have brought a male guest there. "I hope you've kept out of trouble. We've both been worried about you and spoken about you several times. Is everything all right?"

"Not exactly," I equivocated. "I tried one last time to persuade people to look into Anna's death, but I failed. And they weren't happy with me. But as far as I'm concerned, that's their problem, not mine."

She insisted then on making tea. And she produced some scones that she had baked herself. I tucked in, despite everything that had happened, I must confess, and we chatted for quite some time. She reminded me that she had interpreted Anna's letters home as indicating that the relationship with Charlie had become serious, and that she had seemed so happy in the final letters. I talked as discreetly as I could about what I knew of the affair, and I mentioned

Anna's beauty, her attractiveness, and her obvious feelings for Charlie. Then I gradually told her about my final day at the farm, and about my dismissal from the Land Army, which all meant that I could no longer look into her death. She might have been upset if I had rushed into telling her all this, but in the midst of an intimate conversation she accepted it more readily as a confidence and expressed her regret at what the Army had done to me. "You were such a good friend to her. She even said so in her diary, you know."

That stopped me in my tracks. A diary! What diary? I had never seen Anna with a diary.

"You look surprised, but it is what we told you the other day. She would not have wanted you to witness her writing. The diary she kept was returned to us by the Land Army, along with her other things. She mentions you a lot in the pages that I've read. I've not read them all yet."

I asked if I could see the diary. She nodded and went off to get it. I finished my tea and waited, wondering if the diary might contain something that would reveal suddenly what had happened to Anna. It was a quite expensive leather-bound volume that I was handed, with a ribbon bookmarker between the leaves. "Please read as much as you wish," Anna's mother said.

I started at the beginning. There was banal stuff about the farm, milking, trimming hedges, cleaning the dairy, and the other tasks she had been engaged in. I leafed through a few pages. Now she was talking about Charlie. She traced the development of their relationship, he showing interest in her and she uncertain of how to respond. Then, when she agrees to "walk out with him", she discussed the opposition of his parents. All that I knew and I leafed through a few more pages. I now featured in her thoughts, and it was clear that she had found me a little unfriendly. She speculated as to whether I was jealous of her relationship with Charlie, but decided I wasn't. She concluded from something I said that I had been in some trouble before coming to the farm. I again leafed through a few pages. Anna was talking to herself about whether she would "go all the way", the same phrase that she had used with me. I looked up. "You might not want Anna's father to read all this," I said softly.

Her mother looked at me and nodded. "I thought that might be the case. I'll keep it away from him."

Again I flicked past some pages. Now Anna was talking about the difficulties of their first attempt at making love. The diary was nearing the end of the written pages, but I thought that I should pay them more attention. Anna was describing her impressions of that first day of the bombing of North Weald. She wrote about the German fighters and bombers, and the stream of Hurricanes trying to repel them. She expressed her hope that people would be protected by their shelters. And then....why, then she revealed the issue that she had wanted to raise with me. And yes, it was an issue that might have got her killed. My God, I had missed it altogether. This evidence must have been sitting somewhere in our quarters, and I must have been within yards or feet of it half the time I was trying to work out what had happened. If I had spoken to her, I might have prevented her death. A burning pang of guilt ran through me, and I must have gasped and sat back. "What is it, Virginia? What's the matter?"

I let out a long groan of exasperation, mostly with myself. "I should have thought of this," I said. "I should have asked myself more about this. I should have looked through Anna's things for a clue, and this is a clue. I might be able to explain why and how Anna died. But I must get back to Epping."

I showed her the final entry in the diary. She understood the possible implication. I thought quickly and reached into my pocket for Williamson's business card. I asked to use the telephone, but when I got through it turned out that he was not in the office. I put the phone down. I still wanted to go to Epping and to find out the truth, which I now felt was close to me, just asking to be grasped.

"Would you keep calling Scotland Yard and ask for Detective Superintendent Williamson. Explain who you are, and that I've gone back to Epping. Read him those last sentences. If he isn't back by eight o'clock dictate those sentences to someone there and ask them to get them to him. I don't trust anyone else to do anything, but I think he will."

I hurried to leave and to get to Epping, and I wasn't really thinking at all smartly or strategically. I suppose I had received so many rejections that I wanted to pursue this on my own at first. If I envisaged anything, it was Williamson turning up when I had already unmasked the killer. Stupid, stupid me!

I reached Epping before the milk churns had been returned to the farm. That meant that Will had not completed the run that he made each afternoon from the farms to the dairy with the full churns, and then back to the farms with the empty ones from the morning milking. I waited outside the farm. I found a spot where the bit of forest scrubland came down to the roadside. Two yards in and I could sit and watch the road and the entrance to the farm. It was still warm, what people sometimes called an Indian Summer for those September days when the sunshine of August seems to linger. There was little traffic along the road, and only a couple of pedestrians passed me by. Neither noticed me, so I thought I was well camouflaged.

I waited some time, and I had started to think that he must have gone off somewhere else when the loud roar of the engine of his lorry could suddenly be heard. He pulled up at the entrance to the farm and off-loaded the last churns on the back, and then drove the short distance to his house, pulling up in front of the building with a screech. I watched him enter the house and thought that I would have to wait some further time. It was growing dark, and I hoped that if he was going to make a move he would do so soon. I made my way towards the lorry but still hidden by the undergrowth at the side of the road, and I saw a small animal track through which I could get to the lorry. Would I be able to clamber on the back? It had metal fencing that ensured its load stayed on the lorry. Could I scale that? I wasn't sure but I might have to make the effort. After half an hour or so I saw him come out from the house. He was carrying a heavy load which he carefully placed on the passenger seat in the cab. Then he hurried in and out again, pulling a jacket on and eating something from his hand. He climbed up to enter the cab, and that was my cue.

I ran through the gap in the undergrowth and towards the rear of the lorry. As I reached it, it started to move forward, so that the leap I had planned to get my foot onto the platform of the rear of the lorry fell short. I managed to clutch the top of the rail that surrounded the platform, but my feet now trailed along the road as I was dragged by the accelerating vehicle. Will could not see me, and I hoped that he could not sense me clinging on for dear life. I hoped that he would stop soon, and I was fortunate that he did so at the top of the lane that led to the farm. I jumped again and managed this time to get a toehold, so that I could haul myself up and over the metal fencing around the platform. I lay there panting, checking that my feet had survived being dragged along the road. Then I crawled along the platform so that I could shelter myself behind his cab. There was no rear window in the cab, so I was safe from observation. I huddled down and waited whatever developed.

Will drove for quite some time. It grew very dark and he was driving without lights and quite slowly. I supposed he looked for all the world like a delivery driver returning to home late after his day's work. In the final minutes of our journey we went uphill, and our speed dropped still more. Then we pulled off the road and I heard the cab door open. I could see very little from where I was sitting, so I stood up as silently as I could. Still I could see nothing. Will had not come round the back of the lorry at all, but then I smelled the bitter smoke of one of his cigarettes. Perhaps he had just stopped for a break, but I also wondered if he wasn't just checking that he was not overseen. We had reached the top of a hill, and he had found a stopping point in the dark. If he was about to do as I thought he was, he would want to make sure no-one was around. Then I heard a creak from the front of the lorry, as if some door was being opened that was not usually moved. The bonnet, probably, I guessed. The vehicle shuddered a little – Will getting in the non-driver's side of the cab – and dismounting slowly. I waited, though I was sure now what he was doing. But I thought I needed to see him doing his evil worst, so I tiptoed to the rear of the vehicle and climbed back over the rail and down to the ground. I slowly edged along the driver's side of the lorry, and reached the cab, so that in two paces I would be able to see him. But I knew I was perilously close to him. I could hear his movements and the tapping of his messages. I too the last step to where I could peer around the vehicle, and sure enough he was standing by the open bonnet. I could just make out that he had headphones on, and had wired a radio transmitter to the battery of the engine. He was stopping occasionally and shining a torch on a pad that he held up to read. No doubt he had some notes, or he had prepared the full transmission he was making.

I confess to stupidity in my preparation for this spying. I had not thought what I would actually do if I had confirmation of what Anna had guessed at. And as I stood, no doubt gaping in amazement, watching Will at his nasty work, I suddenly realised the gap in my planning. What to do? I didn't know. Not for the first time I cursed myself silently. Should I retreat to the back of the lorry and climb back up, hiding until Will had finished sending his radio message and driven back to Epping? Or should I try to prevent him sending any more information. I realised then that of course I had seen him in North Weald just after the bombing of the airfield. No doubt he would have visited Hornchurch after they were bombed, and the satellite airfields as well, for example at Stapleford. Perhaps there were other airfields too, of which I was not aware or which the pilots Roger and Piotr had not mentioned. How valuable his information must be, immediate and first-hand observation of the results of the Luftwaffe's work. I was so wrapped in these thoughts that I ignored the potential danger that I was in. And that was costly. Something disturbed Will, and he looked around sharply. Even in the dark he must have caught sight of my pale, anxious face. He threw the headphones off and lunged towards me. I turned to flee and, true to form, immediately tripped and fell headlong on the floor. He was on me in seconds, and put his boot firmly on my neck so that my face was shoved into the mud and leaves on the ground. I gasped for breath, and flailed around with my arms and legs, but could not get any hold or grip on him. He seemed to be fumbling in the cab for some reason, when I felt a painful blow on my head. And that was the last thing I felt for some time.

I came round, if that's the right description for being barely conscious, tied up at arms and legs, gagged by a cloth stuffed in my mouth, and lying on my side in what I realised was Will's living room. My head throbbed, my ribs hurt, and my arms and legs were full of prickling sensations where I think the ropes with which I was tied were restricting my blood flow. I groaned, but there was no response. I tried to look around, taking in the small sofa and the table and two chairs that were all I could see of the furniture in the room. It was still dark. Will was not there. I tested the ropes binding my wrists in front of my body. They were too tight even to give the slightest room to wriggle. Similarly my feet, and the ropes extended up to my knees. I must have looked like some overgrown chicken, all trussed for the oven. I heard footsteps, and then felt a kick in my back. I groaned again. "Oh you're awake at last, are you, you bloody meddler? Why the hell didn't you listen to me, and stop trying to play the detective? You're just like that other girl, snooping around me and finding out what I was doing. Should have stuck to that boyfriend of hers, shouldn't she? Well, she won't bother me again, and nor will you once I've worked out what to do with you. Something that will look like another accident, I think, don't you?" He gave me another kick, and I must have passed out, because some time passed. When I woke it was lighter, but there was no sound in the house. I tried to think through the situation. If it was now morning, Will must be on his milk round, picking up churns and delivering them to the dairy, and returning previously used ones to the farms. He would not finish until ten o'clock or shortly after, I estimated. Then he would return to arrange whatever accident he had planned for me. I wondered if Anna's parents had managed to contact Williamson. If they had, what would he do? Call Epping police? They wouldn't do anything, believing it to be just one more figment of my imagination. I hoped that he might do something himself, because the other detectives in Scotland Yard had proved as cynical and disbelieving as their Epping counterparts. They were unlikely to come to my aid. But I couldn't count on him. He might not even have received the message.

I must have slipped in and out of consciousness for some time because I became aware of movements in the living room without having heard Will return home. He was bustling about in another room, and there was a clanking and knocking before he came into the living room. I heard him put something down on the floor, and then he came over and knelt by me. "I've worked it out now," he said in a menacing whisper. "Death by drowning, that's what it'll be. And you'll be found in a pond by the roadside, where you fell off your bike, hitting your head and falling in and drowning while unconscious. Such a sad end!" He stood after this final sneer and kicked me once more in the ribs. I rolled around a little and saw that he had brought an old tin bath into the room. He noticed my look. "Course, you won't drown in the pond itself. That's going to happen right here, where no-one can see." He left me and went into what I assumed was the kitchen, because I heard a tap running and filling some vessel. He returned and poured water into the bath. "I'm going to make some nice muddy water for you to drown in, just like the pond water. So say your prayers now, if that's what you're like." He continued to fetch more water from the kitchen, pouring it into the bath and each time offering me further insults and descriptions of what he was about to do to me. I must confess it weakened me. I was not in the best of health after the various blows and kicks he had aimed at me, both conscious and unconscious, and I could not think how I might escape his clutch when the critical moment came. In fact I could hardly think at all.

Once he had put enough water in the bath, he turned towards me. He grabbed the ropes around my wrists and pulled me to my feet. He started to untie the gag around my mouth. If I could have kicked him I would have done so, but my feet could not move separately, and he still held my wrists tightly. He pulled the cloth out of my mouth, and I tried to scream and shout, though it was a poor effort. My throat was so dry and my mouth so sore that only a half-shout came out. "No-one can hear you here, you silly cow!" he shouted, and slapped me around the face. I stumbled backwards and fell into the sofa. I refused to cry, but the slap had taken all but the last spirit out of me. I saw one opportunity, though, because he had let me go, and I stretched my feet forward towards the handle of the bath, caught it with my toe and raised my feet suddenly, tipping the muddy water straight onto the floor. This time he punched me in the stomach, shoved me onto the floor and retied the gag on my mouth. Then he started to refill the bath. I knew that next time he would take even more care to stop me fighting against him.

Sure enough, when the bath was full he pulled me to my feet again, but this time he punched me twice in the stomach before he removed the gag. I could barely breathe, and shouting was beyond me. I thought I was going to faint. He pulled the gag off and removed the cloth from my mouth again, then he grabbed my hair and twisted my head down towards the bath and the muddy water he had prepared for me. I tried to resist. I tried to shake my body and then my head away from it, but I had no strength left and had given up on life itself. Just as he plunged my face under the water, and I tried not to breathe, there was a crashing sound at the front door. "What the fuck!" he exclaimed and pulling me up he threw me once again onto the sofa. He turned towards the door, but I saw Williamson burst through the door, push Will down while he was off balance, and bring a truncheon crashing down on Will's head twice. Will collapsed on the floor, and Williamson crossed the room to me.

"Are you all right, Miss Beauchamp?" he said, even as he was fumbling to untie the ropes that held my wrists so tightly. He Looked back at Will and saw him move. He crossed the floor to him, and I heard him whisper in Will's ear, "If you move a muscle, I will personally break every bone in your body I can find. And then I'll break the rest." Will stayed where he was. Will had been menacing in his utterances, but Williamson…. well, I had never heard anything so threatening. Williamson went to the kitchen and found a sharp knife, with which he cut the ropes around my legs and feet as I was pulling the final bits of rope off my arms. "I'm sorry it took me so long," he said. "No cars, you see, and no drivers. I had to come here by train. It's ridiculous. I didn't get the message until this morning. Bloody fools the ones who received it first. Didn't realise its significance."

I thought of those last words of Anna's I had read. *I think Will has a radio, one that transmits messages. I saw him carrying it out to his lorry. I must ask Ginny what I should do about it.* The request I had never answered. The words I'd asked her parents to leave for Williamson. He at least had understood their significance. And I cried, horrible, heart-wrenching sobs that came from somewhere deep within me. Williamson held me while I sobbed, but I sensed that he was still watching Will. He was not going to be caught out by any sudden recovery and attempt to escape. I think that he still held the truncheon with which he had beaten Will down. The common police truncheon, that so many comedians had poked fun at in films I had watched. Well, it had been brutally effective in Williamson's hands. He had no compunction in using it.

At that moment there were three more arrivals. Three of the local policemen whom I had met previously came in, took one look at the scene, and then stepped backwards. I think they could see what was coming. Williamson stood up and berated them in a voice of stentorian authority. "Where the bloody hell have you been? I left messages telling you to get here and observe this house hours ago. Your idleness might have led to another murder. What kind of police force do they have in this town? I'm Detective Superintendent

Williamson from Scotland Yard, and I'll be talking to your Chief Constable about the incompetence here.'"

The men looked at Williamson, then at Will, still lying on the floor, and then at me. They may not have understood all of what they saw, but they knew it wasn't good. One of them spoke after there was a hushed pause. "We did not understand the message, sir. We thought it was this young woman stirring things up again."

"Oh you bloody well did, did you? Pity she didn't stir you up before. This man's a murderer." He pointed at Will, using the truncheon to indicate. "So cuff him and get him on his feet. Then one of you had better inform the farmer to come here, and another needs to go and get a vehicle. We'll need to transport him into Central London. I'm taking over the case from you, because you're too bloody incompetent to discover a murderer in your midst."

I had never understood the phrase "jump to it" until I saw those three, who had refused to listen to me and take any action. They couldn't have followed Williamson's orders more quickly! Will was still groggy. Williamson had not shrunk from hitting him very hard. But I was not finished with Will. "Let me…" I muttered, standing up a little shakily.

"What do you want, miss?" Williamson asked.

"Just this," I said as I walked over to where Will was being held. He was awake enough to raise his eyes and look at me with contempt. I had never hit a man, other than playfully, in my life, but I balled my fingers together, pulled my arm back, and before Williamson could stop me, I smashed my fist into his face as hard as I could. He winced, and blood trickled out of his nose. My fingers hurt where I had caught him, but I was not sorry.

"I don't blame you, miss," Williamson said, "but it would probably be better if you didn't do that again."

"I only wanted to do it the once," I replied.

Will cried in a whinging voice, "She can't do that. You stop her." He looked at Williamson with a slight air of defiance.

"Stop resisting arrest, then." Williamson spoke in a quiet but deeply threatening tone. "Otherwise, I may have to take further action." He waved the truncheon in Will's face. Will shook his head and let his eyes look down. Then he pushed Will onto the very sofa where I had only a few minutes before lain helpless and facing death. "Thank you," I blurted out suddenly. "Thank you for coming, for listening, when no-one else would. You did. I don't know why, but you did."

"Perhaps it was because of your father, miss, though I think it's more likely because of you. It sounded as if that other girl's parents were really worried about you. But I was almost too late. I've got to do something about finding a permanent driver. I'm guessing from all the water that's been spilled here that you delayed him, just long enough for me to get here. And that he was going to dump you in a pond somewhere and let us plods think it was an accident again." I nodded. "You've done incredibly well," he added. "A murderer and a spy. And the Murder Squad didn't want to know. You've humiliated them as well as caught that bastard there." He was still using the truncheon to point.

"Excuse my language, miss, but an Englishman reporting to the Jerries about their bombing, that's what's been going on, isn't it? And then murdering young women. No, he's a bastard all right, and I quite understand why you hit him."

We were silent until the policeman returned with Susan. Robert was at a meeting with WarAg, she told us. Williamson told her quickly that Will was the murderer, that he had also nearly killed me after discovering that I knew the truth. Susan was shocked, genuinely so, and she almost went for Will herself. She certainly came out with language that I had never heard her use before. Williamson allowed her the rant, and then asked her to take me to the farmhouse, give me sweet tea and some food, and allow me to clean myself up. She put her arms around me, almost the first time she had shown any such gesture, and led me away along the lane and into the kitchen of the house. I drank some tea and ate some bread and cheese that she gave me and went to the bathroom. On my face were some marks that looked like those I had seen on Anna's dead face. I shuddered to think how close I had come to joining her. Being impetuous, and not planning things, those were my faults, and not for the first time I vowed to myself not to do things so thoughtlessly. I washed my face and dried myself off. I noticed that my wrists were red and sore where the ropes had gripped me, and I went back and asked Susan for some ointment. She applied some herself and gave me the remainder. I asked where Charlie was, and she said that he was doing some hedging work at one of the far ends of the farm. She would tell him what Williamson had said as soon as he returned. Then she suggested that I lie down in the living room, and I did so, falling asleep very quickly.

It was Williamson who woke me some time later. "We've packed him off to Scotland Yard," he said, "and I've called Anna's parents on the telephone and told them that we've found Anna's killer, and that you are safe. I agreed to go there tomorrow and explain everything. Now I've got to get you home and go back and start questioning him. So I've got a car outside ready." I noted that he would not even name Will. I think he despised him deeply, both for what he had done to Anna and for being a spy.

The car sped through the green areas of forest and grassland that led into the suburbs, and I watched everything go by as if I were still in a daze. Williamson made a few remarks as we travelled, but I was monosyllabic in my replies. I think I was still experiencing some kind of shock. As we reached the city, however, I came around a little. I asked what would happen to Will. Williamson said that he would question him, but that he would almost certainly be joined by a government security and intelligence officer. They would need to find out how he had been recruited, and who else he knew was working with the Germans. They would go over all that he had discovered while driving around, and what he had sent to the enemy by way of information. "He must have been a mine of useful information to them while they were planning the attacks on the airfields. He's responsible for a major leak of war secrets. And murder of course. So at the end of it he will be tried, but almost certainly in secret. The government does not like to admit to such leaks in public. You might be needed as a witness in the trial, and I will have to take a statement from you in the coming days."

"And after all that?" I asked, though I knew the answer.

"The judges may take into account any assistance he gives us, but his crimes are so serious that I think he will be executed. Murder and treason. If it was peacetime you'd be a national heroine. As it is, I am telling people mostly that Will is a murderer. I'm not going to tell anyone else, other than Anna's parents and those at the farm, about the detail of what he was. And only a few people in the Yard will be told. So I'd be grateful if you would keep a lid on it. Tell your father, though, so he knows what you've been through."

As we came nearer to Scotland Yard he asked me if I would like to come with him to Anna's parents the next day. I agreed without hesitation. He said that he would reserve a car, but that he might find it difficult to obtain a driver. He suggested, therefore, that I might drive the car if I felt up to it, though he said he knew I needed a good night's sleep. I was pleasantly surprised by the suggestion. It was months since I had last been behind the wheel, and I enjoyed driving.

The car took me home. The apartment was empty, which was no surprise. My father and Henri seemed to be away more than they were at home. There was some food in the kitchen, though, and signs that Henri had been there in my absence. I had a bath, albeit a shallow one to save water, ate some food and went to bed. My dreams were troubled at first, and I woke up twice in a panic, but then I fell into a deeper sleep.

CHAPTER 22
SEPTEMBER 7ᵀᴴ 1940

I was sore, both physically and spiritually I think, when I awoke. So much had happened to me in such a short space of time that I felt exhausted, even though I had slept well for some hours. I also realised that I had not seen Piotr during the last critical days and vowed to correct that as soon as possible. I dressed and had breakfast simultaneously, bringing bread and jam and tea into my bedroom and consuming them while I sorted out some fresh clothes. I caught a bus heading for the general direction of Scotland Yard. The bus was full, as was usual in those days, and I was crammed between a middle-aged man who certainly needed a bath, and a mother with two bawling children. I felt sorry for her, though I could have wished they were further away from me. My head still hurt, and my make-up had not disguised all the marks on my face. They probably wished themselves further away from me.

At Scotland Yard I had to sit and wait a while for Williamson. The uniformed sergeant at the desk looked at me a while, and then in a quiet moment approached me. "Excuse me, miss," he said politely, "but are you the young woman who discovered that murderer brought in yesterday?"

I had not expected this information to have become such common currency. I thought I would have to let Williamson know. "Yes, I suppose I am, because he tried to murder me as well as my friend." I didn't want to say any more.

The sergeant leaned towards me. "Bloody good work," he spoke in a quiet voice. He nodded his head as if in agreement with himself. "Yes, bloody well done."

"I don't think the detective in charge wants very much said about it," I whispered back.

"You're right, of course, but I just wanted to tell you how well you've done. Bloody good work to catch a bastard like that when no-one here would believe you."

When Williamson came down and guided me to where the car was parked, I told him of the sergeant's little speech. He laughed at first and was then a little cross. "The trouble is," he confided in me, "there's always some tension between uniform and non-uniform. Uniform think non-uniform are stuck-up and feel they're superior, and non-uniform think the others are plods, foot soldiers who are beneath them in status. So when one lot mucks up, and there is no doubt that non-uniform mucked up here, the other side gloats about it when they find out. I will need to get someone in top brass to issue a memo forbidding any discussion of the case. It won't shut everyone up, but it will quieten things down."

When we reached the car he explained that he'd obtained special permission for me to drive the car, and he'd explained to his superiors the reasons why we were going out to Romford. He asked me to drive fairly speedily – he couldn't give me permission to break any speed limits – so that we could get the business done. While I drove, which I enjoyed once I'd got accustomed to the car's rather sticky gear change, which renewed some of the pains in my back from the kicks I had received, he told me that Will had confessed to him and the security officer a great deal already. No doubt, he explained, he was trying to save his skin, but in the process he had revealed that he had been recruited by a member of the German Embassy staff before the war, when he had attended a fascist sympathisers' meetings. He had told them where and what he did as a job, and they had thought he would be valuable. He had radioed information about six airfield bases and was busy reporting on the damage inflicted by the raids. He had also given Williamson the names of three other possible spies from the meetings he had attended, though he did not know where they lived. He was due to face a further grilling later that day from the security branch. He had been charged with murder and attempted murder and would probably be charged with treason that evening. A secret trial would then be held within two weeks. The normal course of justice, which would have lasted some months, would not apply in this case. The security people might, he thought, be considering sending some false messages, if they thought that he was telling them the correct calling codes. But there were enormous risks, which might dissuade them.

Williamson went on to ask me about the Land Army and where I stood with them. I told him that they had dismissed me, though I now realised that it was possible I could appeal against that decision, given that it was based on my questioning about Anna's death. I confessed that I was not sure that I was well-matched to the Army. They seemed to want compliance to all their instructions, and falling in with silly rules, but when you considered that the Girls were all really adults, or almost all were, it seemed more like school again, as one of my companions had said when we first saw Raines Hall. I could not immediately see an alternative. I told him about failing my medical because of having had, or having had some contact with, TB. He said that he was sorry that I had not been able to serve in the way I wished, and asked if I might seek an administrative role somewhere in government, to help with the war cause. I said that I did not have any secretarial skills, and that I could not see myself happily filing papers and making tea for the men making the important decisions. He smiled and said he could understand my reluctance there.

We came to a section of open, wide road. Williamson looked at his watch and said we were running a little late. He asked me to speed up, and when I did so, to speed up a bit more. I didn't mind. In the very last years in Poland my father had allowed me to deliver some of the cars he had imported or built there. One or two were very fast indeed. I enjoyed the sensation of speed, and now put my foot down hard. But I was still able to slow down and fall in behind a tractor that was hauling a trailer of hay between the fields that the road bordered, and again to slow down when I saw an oncoming vehicle overtaking a bus. "You've obviously driven a lot previously, miss," Williamson said. I told him about Poland but confessed that I had not driven much in England recently because of the rationing of petrol, and because my father was away so often. He became silent and seemed to be mulling something over. Then he spoke. "I may be able to help you with doing something to help the country." I looked up with interest and then returned my attention to the road. "I've talked this over in the Yard, and they've agreed that I can ask you to become my driver. They know that my eyes stop me from driving, and that I'm now constantly frustrated by having to reserve a driver in advance or to use public transport, however difficult the route is. So I told them that you might be available. They said that you would be enlisted as a Special and would have to follow all the rules and regulations. I assured them that you would have no difficulty with that." He smiled as he said this, and that made me smile too. "You would drive me wherever I need to go, and I know that they are considering giving me responsibilities that will mean I'm travelling in London virtually every day. But I think you could do an extra job for me and be my eyes and ears in situations where I am not able to ask questions. You've proved yourself already.

You'll be the first Special they've recruited who's already fingered a murderer and a spy!"

I was surprised. Then I realised. "So has my driving you today been some kind of audition?" He confessed to this but said that he had needed to find out if I could drive at speed. So, yes, he had slightly deceived me. But he had not wanted to discuss the job with me, only then to say no if he found I was not able to drive quickly but safely. He asked me to think it over, and to ask any questions that came to mind. So I was slightly distracted in my driving, but I found my way to Anna's parents with just one need to reroute after taking a wrong turning.

Anna's parents had other visitors than us. The Land Army had obviously heard about Anna being murdered, not killed in an accident, and the two committee members I had assailed at her funeral were now in the parlour drinking tea from the best china in the house. They were intrigued by Williamson, but when they saw who his driver was, they were more than a little abashed. "Miss Beauchamp," one of them greeted me, "what a pleasant surprise to see you." I could have been sick at the hypocrisy of her. I declined to shake her hand, and instead hugged each of Anna's parents.

Her mother held my shoulders and scanned my face. With one hand she traced what I knew were the outlines of bruising. She looked at my wrists, which were still red from the ropes that had been drawn around them. She sensed that my back and ribs were sore, and then she kissed me firmly on the cheek. "Thank you," she said as she held me close. "Thank you so much for what you've done. But you should never have risked things so much. You seem to have suffered for it." I nodded, but Williamson interrupted us.

"This young woman has been quite remarkable," he said, "in discovering an evil murderer when no-one would believe her." He paused and looked at the two Land Army committee members. I think he was a bit of an actor, really. He knew how to use a dramatic pause. "I've more to tell you, but I'm afraid that these two ladies will have to wait outside while I do so. There are things that are only for your ears." They tried to protest, but he insisted, and would not accept them waiting in the hallway beyond the room. He made them go into the back garden. Then he returned to Anna's parents. "Anna was a war heroine, you need to know that. What I'm about to tell you, you are not allowed to repeat because it's a war secret." Anna's mother looked astonished, and I took her arm and guided her to a seat. "The man who murdered her was a spy for the Germans." Anna's father exclaimed at this but could hardly put his thoughts into words. He sat down next to his wife. "Yes, it's true. He drove a lorry around Essex and Hertfordshire, and he was reporting to the Germans about the airfields, and then about the results of the attacks on the airfields. You know from her diary, the extract that Miss Beauchamp had you dictate to the clerk at the Yard, that she thought he had a transmitter. She was trying to confirm that when he saw her and decided instantly that he would have to kill her to keep his secret. Miss Beauchamp here almost suffered exactly the same fate just yesterday morning. That's why she's more than a bit bruised and sore. He knocked Anna out, and later, in the dark, carried her into the barn and threw her down. I'm so sorry about your loss, but she encountered someone evil, a traitor, who will pay for his crimes. And I will recommend Anna for a civilian award, from the King. She deserves that, though they may delay awarding anything simply because all this is a war secret. The government does not like talking about spies. They think it's bad for morale. But I thought you had a right to know. That's why we're here today."

Anna's parents were stunned, obviously. Neither could speak, and they looked first at one another and then back at Williamson and me. "Superintendent," Amma's father finally said, "we are very, very grateful that you've come and told us all this. And Miss Beauchamp, we cannot praise you enough for having persevered in this when all were against you, including I think the two ladies from the Land Army. We are just so thankful that you have survived this, while we regret that poor Anna had to be the one to discover the truth about this Nazi sympathiser. You were the one who could not accept that Anna's death was an accident, and you have vindicated Anna by your persistence."

I think we were all close to tears at this point, and there was a slightly awkward silence, which Anna's mother broke by offering to make more tea, though she nudged her husband to get Williamson "something a little bit stronger". I followed her into the kitchen and assisted in the tea-making, and she was able to say to me, "He doesn't know about Anna and Charlie, well, all the detail anyway, so if you can stop the Superintendent referring to that it would be good." I assured her of the Superintendent's discretion but said that I would mention it on our journey back. I also told her that Williamson had said that Will's trial would be held in secret, so no-one would learn anything of Anna's relationship with Charlie. It was not the focus of the trial, which would be her having seen the radio transmitter. She again thanked me, and loaded the crockery and the teapot on a large tray which she invited me to carry in. With Williamson's agreement the two Land Army ladies were allowed back in, though they tried to stand on their dignity and wondered aloud if it had really been necessary to exclude them. "Yes it was," Anna's father said with finality in his voice, and they had to accept it. They turned to me, however.

"Miss Beauchamp," one of them said, "we've talked the situation over and we would like you to resume your Land Army duties. We wondered, though, whether you would like to return to Raines Hall rather than continue at Houblions. It must have some bad memories for you." It was tempting. To resume my close friendship with Lewi was very tempting. The companionship was something I craved, I knew that about myself.

Williamson was listening to what was said, however. "You need to know that I have myself offered Miss Beauchamp a job with the Metropolitan Police, as a Special Constable. She is thinking that offer over even now."

The Committee ladies bridled at that. "But Miss Beauchamp is a Land Girl, a member of the Army. She took a pledge to serve the Land Army."

"But you dismissed her," Williamson said firmly. "Which means that she is free to choose."

My mind was racing. I wanted to serve the country as best I could, and I hoped that whatever I did would prove my abilities and lead on to something more. That's why I'd agreed to join the Land Army in the first place. But I had been dismissed from the Army, and that dismissal would stand against my record. Alongside the two school expulsions, the visit to the Magistrates, and my TB. So what should I do?

I turned to the two ladies. "I think I would like to take the job with the police. It probably suits my temperament better. But I need you to remove my dismissal from my record. That was unfair, as I think has been proved by events."

The two ladies hesitated. Then one said, "I don't see how we can do that if you won't come back to the Land Army. Dismissal is just that, dismissal."

Williamson was clearly annoyed by this refusal, but he was diplomatic. "I'm sure that you can re-enlist Miss Beauchamp, and then discharge her to the service of the Metropolitan Police. After all, you wouldn't want it widely discussed that the Land Army had dismissed a woman who had unmasked a murderer, because she was asking awkward questions about it. That would not look very good if it got in the papers."

It was a cunning threat. Williamson had not said that he would tell the newspapers himself, but his words carried that promise. "You wouldn't…" gasped one of the two, but the other gave her a firm dig in the ribs and interrupted. "No, we would not want that to appear in the papers. So, yes, we will wipe out the dismissal, and then honourably discharge Miss Beauchamp to you. Will that do?"

Williamson beamed, and I was pleased with the outcome. I was not at all sure what I'd let myself in for, and part of me regretted that I would not be with Lewi again. That was a blow, but I could always preserve our friendship in other ways. And I knew it was best if I did not encounter the rule of Miss Capthorn again. It could only end badly. The two Land Army ladies looked aggrieved, but they were forced to comply by Williamson's veiled threat. Anna's parents were obviously pleased by the outcome, though when we parted I could tell that there was still a deep sadness there. Her mother again hugged me tightly and asked me to stay in touch with them. She hinted that she felt close to Anna through me, because I had shared lodgings with her, had discovered her dead body, and revealed the evil that had overtaken her. I promised that I would visit again and share more about the work we had done on the farm.

As I started the car I asked if there was time for us to visit Epping quickly. I wanted to square things up with the family, and to collect my cycle, if I could retrieve it from wherever it was. Williamson agreed, and I drove through the early autumn countryside to the farm. Everywhere I saw that the harvesting of wheat and hay was complete, and that farmers were now turning to gathering fruit and lifting vegetables from the ground. The chestnut trees by the roadside were starting to brown, and to drop their red-brown nuts. It was a warm, sunny day and Williamson asked me to lower my window while he rolled his down, to air the car.

When we reached the farm I drove through to the yard, and both Susan and Robert came out. Their greeting me was unlike anything they had done in the months I had worked there, with both of them hugging me and thanking me. I had not been feted so much in one day since my eighteenth birthday, and I wondered what lay behind it. Robert explained: "Once we knew what had happened yesterday we had a long family discussion. Charlie has agreed not to enlist until at least this time next year. We've now been promised two new Land Girls so that we can train them up, and I've agreed with WarAg how many fields to plough up. I can keep two-thirds of the herd through next year, though there may be a further change next September. Charlie is doing the run with the churns in the short term, but I think we'll be able to find someone to take it on. The lorry is ours, and the house will be vacant, so it should be straightforward. Charlie is still upset that he did not understand what had happened to Anna, but he's grateful to you that you kept worrying away at it."

Williamson spoke to them next, and he informed them about the war secret he was about to reveal. He explained it all in similar terms to our earlier discussion at Anna's parents, and he warned them off telling others about Will's activities. Just as he was finishing, Charlie and Katherine came into the yard carrying the long-handled spades used for digging out trenches and ditches. He too did not hesitate but came up and hugged and thanked me. "That argument you had with us in the yard," he said, "it made me think, and realise how stupid I had been. I had ignored things that I could and should have noticed, and I apologise for anything I've said to you when I was so wrong about it all."

I told him about our visit to Anna's parents, and I suggested to him that he could go and see them, and that they liked to hear more about Anna. Then I drew him aside and I whispered to him that Anna's mother had some idea about how deep his relationship with Anna had been, but that her father perhaps did not. I felt I was honouring what she had asked of me in telling Charlie this. Where previously he would have blasted me for being so bold, he was again thankful. He promised to visit them and to be careful what he said. But he would tell them how much they had loved one another.

I turned and asked about my cycle. Robert said that they had rescued it yesterday, and he fetched it from the barn. Williamson took it and tied it to the car with some rope that was in the boot. I said my farewells, and we set off on the road into London.

It was around four-thirty as we drove along the old Newmarket coaching road, and I was enjoying the drive and the warmth of the air, thinking that everything had worked out as well as it could in such tragic circumstances, when Williamson suddenly told me to pull over. I was surprised but did as he asked and pulled into a layby. He got out and crossed the road, but turned back to look in a southward direction, shading his eyes from the late afternoon sun. I could hear a droning sound coming from that direction, so I too climbed out and crossed the road. It was a frightening sight. Squadrons of bombers could be seen just a few miles away, heading westwards towards London. On their flanks and above them were hundreds of fighters, obviously there to protect the bombers. Some other fighter planes, ours I guessed, were trying to harass this flying swarm. This was the sight and sound that every Londoner had dreaded for months, and it was shocking, because the number of bombers was simply staggering – there were hundreds of them! They were indeed like a flight of deadly insects, ones which had seen their target and were aiming straight for their victim. I had never seen so many aircraft in the sky together. The line of planes as they passed us seemed to go back to the horizon. "They're following the Thames, the bastards," muttered Williamson. We watched in silence for a while, then he said, "We'll go to Chigwell. There's a point there where we can see what's going on."

He guided me in driving through Buckhurst Hill and part of Chigwell, two village-cum-suburbs that were set in Essex but whose inhabitants mostly worked in London. On a hilltop there we found a viewing place that showed the whole of east London. We were not the only people there. Those who had gathered were in the same horrified silent state as us. As we looked across the miles of buildings that lay between us and the City we started to see small flashes of light. It was the bombs falling. One or two exploded in much larger, terrifying bursts of light, and then died back to what must have been burning fires. Despite the distance one particularly violent explosion was followed some seconds later by a booming sound. I felt sick at heart at the thought of what was happening. I could see it but do nothing at all about it. Then some guns on the ground started to fire upwards, and we could see the small flashes in the sky as the shells exploded.

Williamson turned to me, seeing my horror. "It's shocking, I know. Hitler has brought the front of the war right to us, and that's the East End that's taking all the blows. It's what we all feared. And I know that war brings out the best in humans sometimes, but also the worst. We're going to have our work cut out. Are you sure you've made the right decision?"

I thought for a while. I had rejected the opportunity to stay working on the land, and to be reunited with my friend. I would have enjoyed relative safety. I had instead embraced working for the police in what was now a battlefront, besieged city. But I knew it was what I needed to do. I nodded. "I'm sure," I said.

It was September 7th 1940. Black Saturday. The day the Blitz on London really started, and I joined the forces trying to combat its effects.